RESCUE

A SCI-FI ALIEN WARRIOR ROMANCE

BARBARIANS OF THE SAND PLANET
BOOK TEN

TANA STONE

BROADMOOR BOOKS

NOTE FROM THE AUTHOR

This book first appeared in the charity anthology Pets in Space 8 and is relatively unchanged from that version (aside from one extra chapter). Thanks so much for reading!

Tana Stone

CHAPTER
ONE

"You sure you're up for it?" The Zevrian security chief glanced back at Tegan as she led her onto the spaceship, her boots making the metal ramp shake and rattle. "Have you ever handled four pregnant women at one time?"

Tegan stopped twirling a strand of chestnut hair around her pointer finger as she met Tori's gaze. "They aren't all due at the same time, are they?"

"No, we aren't."

Tegan blanched, her steps faltering. "I didn't know you were one of the expecting mothers."

Tori dismissed her mistake with a wave of one hand as she reached the top of the ship's ramp. "Don't sweat it. Zevrians don't show our pregnancies until we're almost ready to pop, and then we almost literally pop. Our babies are born through our stomachs." The alien with brown skin and a row of bumps along her hairline turned to the new midwife she'd just hired. "I should have asked you if you have experience with Zevrian births."

"I've assisted with one," Tegan admitted, "but I've delivered hundreds of healthy babies, so I feel confident about taking care of the four moms-to-be on this ship."

Tori nodded and eyed her quickly. "Good. I'm hoping you also have tricks to keep the babies from driving us crazy once they're here."

"I thought the job was only for the deliveries."

Tori gave her a crooked grin that exposed her pointed, back teeth. "It is. I was joking. I know there will be no way to keep a half-Zevrian, half-Dothvek baby under control, but if all goes according to plan, we'll be back on the Dothvek home world by the time I deliver. My mate's tribe lives in tents in a desert. Babies' cries don't echo as much out there." She gestured to the steel ceiling of the spaceship. "In here, it's enough to drive you mad."

"How many babies are already on board?"

"Only two, but one is half Lycithian shapeshifter, so be warned. Qek thinks it's hilarious to shift into the form of Pog."

Tegan wasn't sure if this was another joke, but Tori wasn't smiling. "Is Pog the other baby?"

Tori snorted out a laugh. "I wish. Pog is a Lycithian shapeshifting glurkin." When she didn't respond, Tori added, "A pet."

Tegan frowned. She wasn't a fan of animals on spaceships. Actually, she didn't have any experience with animals on spaceships. She wasn't a fan of animals anywhere. The only creatures that had lived among the settlers on the dingy outpost she'd grown up on had been scavenging grinder-wolves. They were mangy beasts who would as soon take a chunk from your leg as look at you, so she'd learned to steer clear. "How big of a pet?"

Tori held her hands out and apart as if she were holding a

small sugar melon. "Not big, and I'm pretty sure he's ninety percent green fur."

"Small and green." Tegan made a mental note. "Got it."

Tori held up a finger as she hung a right and led Tegan down a corridor. "But be warned, a green ball of fluff could be Qek pretending to be Pog."

Tegan took all this in, wondering suddenly if she'd made a mistake. When Tori had approached her stall in the marketplace, she'd been sure the tough-looking female was lost. Nothing about the Zevrian with wild, dark curls held on top of her head by a pair of sharp, metal sticks conveyed that she'd be interested in Tegan's natural remedies, but then she'd made her proposition. Join the bounty hunter babes—that was the phrase she'd used—on their ship until all the females aboard gave birth. In exchange, she'd be paid handsomely, along with her room and board.

The credits she'd been promised weren't the reason Tegan had said yes to the odd proposal. It was true she was an experienced midwife, and taking care of four pregnant females would be a breeze compared to her usual workload. Babies seemed to come with brutal frequency in the far-flung outpost, so there was rarely a week she didn't deliver at least one, usually more. The money Tori had promised would more than compensate her for her work and her time, but it was the chance to travel among the stars that had been the reason Tegan had said yes without thinking.

Not only did she want to experience space travel, but she also wanted to get away from the place she'd lived for her entire life. She'd been born into poverty to a single mother on the outpost, and every day of her life had been a struggle to stay afloat. She supposed she was luckier than most. Her mother had taught her how to be a midwife, so she had a skill that was in steady demand, but it was also a job that made her feel like nothing ever changed.

Babies continued to be born without fathers, since most men on the outpost ended up leaving for better opportunities or were only ever passing through. The mothers struggled, children often went hungry, and young women eyed handsome visitors as a means to an escape the squalor. So, the cycle continued.

Tegan scanned the dark interior of the ship, her heart hammering. But she was finally doing it. She was leaving. Even if it was only for a while.

"I didn't expect a group called the bounty hunter babes to have such a battleship," she admitted as they wound down another dimly lit corridor.

"This wasn't always our ship." Tori glanced back and grinned at her. "It's actually a Zevrian mercenary ship we...acquired."

It sounded like there was a story there, but before she could ask, something bumped her leg, and she jumped. The green ball of fur scampering around her legs made a series of high-pitched sounds.

"Speak of the devil," Tori muttered as she paused. "That's Pog." She bent to get a better look. "I'm almost positive it's Pog."

Despite her usual fear of animals, Tegan smiled at the little creature. How could she be afraid of something so small? She couldn't even see any teeth. She reached down and ruffled the fur on the top of his head. At least, she thought it was the top of his head. It was hard to tell since he seemed to be completely round and rolled around a lot.

"Uh oh." Tori gave her a sympathetic look as Pog's noises turned into purrs. "Now you've done it."

Tegan snatched back her hand. "What have I done?"

"You've made him purr. Now, he's never going to leave you alone." Tori shook her head. "Bexli is so busy with her son that she doesn't spend as much time with Pog, which means he's a bit attention starved. I hope you were looking for a new best friend."

Tori started walking again and Tegan followed, but true to Tori's words, the little green puff followed close at her heels. She found herself slowing down so he could keep up, but that meant she was falling behind, so Tegan scooped up Pog in one arm and then jogged to catch up to the Zevrian.

Tori didn't look back as she proceeded through an arched doorway, and Tegan stopped short once she followed her through.

They were on the ship's bridge, which had not been what she'd been expecting. The ship in general wasn't what she'd anticipated from a team of bounty hunters who called themselves babes. The dark interior was almost cave-like, and it felt like a serious war ship. Not at all like vessel filled to the brim with pregnant females.

"You're back!" A woman with curly, blonde hair spun around in a captain's chair, her smile flickering when she spotted Tegan. "With a friend."

"She's not a friend." Tori jerked a thumb behind her. "This is Tegan, our new midwife." She swept an arm toward the woman in the chair. "This is Danica, the ship's captain."

Tegan gave the captain a small wave before she briefly scanned the half-moon-shaped space that was dotted with black consoles, and boasted a long wall of glass that overlooked the dusty shipyard. Aside from the blonde, there was a woman at a console with straight, black hair pulled up in a high ponytail, and two massive, gold-skinned aliens with plenty of tattoos, wearing nothing but leather pants.

"You found one?" Danica stood and released an audible sigh. "Good work, Tor."

The other woman twisted at her console and put a hand on her small baby bump. "Welcome aboard. I'm Caro, the ship's pilot."

One of the gold aliens stepped forward, and Tegan's gaze was drawn to the cuffs of tattooed symbols ringing his impressive biceps. "I am Vrax, Tori's mate."

"I am T'Kar," the other alien said. His tattoos were on his chest, and were more intricate, like an elaborate breastplate of ink. "My mate is Holly, the ship's engineer. You will meet her soon."

"Because she's about to burst," Tori muttered.

"We're so happy you agreed to join us," Danica said, walking toward Tegan with a wide smile. "We've been searching for a traveling midwife for a while. We don't want to have to return to the Dothvek home world for each birth." Then her gaze drifted to the ball of fur tucked in Tegan's arm. "Is that Pog?"

"He's found a new best friend," Tori said.

"Better than you?" Caro teased the Zevrian.

"Ha ha." Tori wrinkled her brow and eyed Pog. "Let's just hope this means he stops leaving pellets on my bed."

Tegan glanced down at the fur ball that was purring so loud he was vibrating as she held him. This was a very strange ship.

TWO

"Did you hear about the new crew mate?"

Zaandr glanced up at his friend Rixx who was laying in the bunk above his. Since he was Dothvek and blessed by the goddesses with the ability to sense the emotions and thoughts of his fellow Dothveks, he could tell that his best friend wasn't actually interested in his answer. Rixx already knew he hadn't.

"There is a new member of the crew?" Then he picked up on a detail in Rixx's thoughts. "But not a warrior. A female."

Rixx swung his legs over the side of the bunk. "Tori brought her on when we stopped at that small outpost. She's here to deliver the babies."

Zaandr frowned. On their home world, the priestesses brought the babies into the world. But they were not on his home planet anymore, a fact that he was still getting used to.

He and Rixx *had* been the newest additions to the bounty hunting crew. They'd joined the ship when it had returned to the Dothvek world to retrieve Dev and Trek, twin Dothveks who'd rescued a human woman and made her their mate.

With all the babies due on the ship, the bounty hunters needed warriors to fill in for the posts that would soon be vacated, if only for a short while.

Zaandr had been lucky. Vrax, who was Tori's mate, was his half-brother, and had vouched for his skills navigating across the sands by the stars. He'd suggested Zaandr join the ship as a navigator.

Rixx had been even more lucky because he'd been Zaandr's best friend since childhood. The two were so inseparable that Vrax had rolled his eyes and said that Rixx could join, if he agreed to learn everything there was to know about engineering. So, Zaandr had spent his time on the bridge learning how to translate the rudimentary navigational skills that worked so well on the sands to the ship's technology, and Rixx had been by Holly's side in the engine room as she taught him how the complex ship worked.

They only saw each other when they returned to their small quarters to rest between shifts, or when they sat together for meals. Still, it was Zaandr's dream come true to journey to the stars—something he'd never imagined possible before the bounty hunters crash landed on his planet—and he didn't care how hard he had to work.

"So, she's not permanent, either?" Zaandr asked.

Rixx jumped down from the top bunk, his thoughts hot with questions. *What do you mean?*

Zaandr thought about correcting his friend. They'd been told to limit the amount they communicated without talking since they were now living among those who weren't able to hear thoughts and sense emotions. But it was hard not to slip into the mental shorthand he and Rixx had acquired over their lifetime. He swung his own legs to the floor. "We came on board to fill positions while the females are recovering from childbirth and spending time with their new babies. That need will fade."

Rixx shook his head. "I disagree, brother. A ship this size needs a larger crew. We have empty cabins as it is." Then he cocked an eyebrow. "And have you seen the way our Dothvek brothers look at their mates? It will not be long before they are heavy with child again."

Zaandr's face warmed at the suggestion, and Rixx laughed, picking up on his discomfort quickly. "Still shy around human women?"

It wasn't only human women, Zaandr thought. Even though he was as big and brawny as any Dothvek warrior, he'd never felt the brash confidence that Rixx did around females. His friend had been known to charm a Dothvek priestess-in-training out of her robes, while he had only experienced one fumbling encounter with a female.

It wasn't that he didn't desire females. He did. But they provoked in him the hammering of his heart and the jangle of his pulse.

Rixx dropped a heavy hand on his bare shoulder. "Do not worry yourself, Zan. Between our work schedule and her delivering babies, we probably won't even see the new female much."

Zaandr let out a relived breath and hated himself for it. He was a trained Dothvek warrior who had made it through the *tahadu*, the coming-of-age gauntlet that every Dothvek warrior had to endure. He was deadly with a blade and was a skilled hunter on the sands. There was little on the Dothvek home world that frightened him. But he wasn't there anymore.

"Come." Rixx grabbed his hand and hoisted him to his feet. "We should go to the kitchens before it is time to work again. I know it isn't time for our group meal, but maybe there is still some of the grilled meat that we brought on board with us."

Zaandr nodded. The humans weren't as fond of the pungent meat that was roasted over a spit in their oasis village, so the supply of it they'd brought with them hadn't dwindled as fast as expected. That, and it had such a strong smell that none of the pregnant females could be in the same room as it. Or, he'd heard, kiss their mate if he'd eaten it, which meant it had been left to him and Rixx to consume.

His mouth watered as they left their quarters and made their way to the kitchens, winding through the tight corridors that were dimly lit. The floor rumbled beneath their feet, the constant reminder they were flying through space, but the sensation no longer startled Zaandr. The jerk in the rumbling did, though.

Rixx stopped quickly, holding up a hand. "That's not a normal sound for the engines."

Zaandr was impressed by how fast his friend had picked up the sounds and motions of the ship. Holly had been teaching him to listen to the ship as if he were on the sands back home, and he'd done just that. Now, he could decipher every creak and jolt.

Are you sure? Zaandr asked, too shocked to remember to speak aloud.

He moved his head up and down, his expression grim. *I need to get to the engine room.*

Zaandr watched him rush off, concern tickling the back of his brain. He brushed it aside. Aside from that initial jolt, there had been nothing. Even if there was an issue, Rixx and Holly could fix it. That, he knew.

Even so, he was no longer in the mood for salty, roasted meat. But he also didn't want to return to his quarters alone. Turning, Zaandr headed for the bridge. It wasn't his shift yet, but he didn't mind getting in some extra study time at the navigational console.

He picked up his pace as he thought about studying the stars, rounding a corner, and running smack into someone. She was also moving fast, so she bounced off his chest. Zaandr had to reach out fast to grab her arms so she wouldn't fall backward. There was a yelp and a then a chirp. Two someones?

"I'm so sorry." The female peered at him, her brown hair falling back from her face. Then she looked down at the green fur-ball tucked in the crook of one arm. "Are you okay, Pog?"

Zaandr wrinkled his brow at her in confusion. Was this the new crew mate? Why was she carrying around Bexli's shape-shifting pet?

"I'm new," the woman said. "You must be...?"

It took Zaandr a beat to realize she was waiting for him to tell her his name. "Zaandr. I'm also new to the ship, but not as new as you."

"Hi, not-as-new Zaandr. I'm Tegan."

He nodded. "I heard you were on board to help with all the babies."

She raised her eyebrows then narrowed her gaze. "You're not one of the fathers, are you?"

His eyes popped wide. The thought of touching one of his fellow Dothveks' mates made his face burn. "Me? One of the fathers? No!"

She gave him a half smile. "So that's a no?"

He opened his mouth, but then he got the strong sense that she was teasing him.

Tegan stepped back. "I might not be seeing you much then, Zaandr, but it was nice to meet you."

He nodded mutely as she scooted by him, cursing himself for sounding so foolish. At least she was right. He probably would get very few occasions to embarrass himself with her again.

THREE

Tegan eyed the very pregnant woman sitting on the platform in the medical bay. Her belly was like a giant balloon protruding in front of her as she rubbed one hand over it then scratched absently.

"So, can you do anything about it?"

"Max, right?"

The woman flicked her other hand through her short, dark hair and met Tegan's gaze with wide, blue eyes. "That's right. Technically, it's Maxine but no one calls me that. Technically, I'm also a doctor but not a medical doctor, and I know nothing about anatomy or childbirth. My specialty is minerals." She blew out a breath. "Not much help when you're growing a person inside you."

Tegan ran her hands over the swollen belly and smiled. "The baby is big and very active."

"You're telling me." Max managed a weak smile. "It's half Dothvek."

"Are you in pain?"

Max shook her head. "No, but I have to pee all the time and breathing is not easy."

"Unfortunately, that's normal at this stage." Tegan walked to the cabinets inset in the walls and opened them. Although, the ship was decently stocked with standard medical supplies, they didn't have any of the herbal remedies that Tegan preferred. Luckily, she'd brought some with her, but after a few days tending to the very pregnant women on the ship, she'd almost run out.

She snagged a small bottle, holding the brown glass up to the light to see that there were only a few drops left in the bottom. She twisted off the cap and emptied the remaining oil into her palm. She slid her hands under the hem of Max's shirt.

"Will that stop me from peeing every time I sneeze?" Max lowered her voice. "I'm running out of clean underwear."

Tegan laughed as she shook her head. "Sadly, it won't. I've never heard of a healing oil that will fix that. This will help with the itching, though. It will help your skin stretch naturally so you won't get marks."

Max let out a sigh. "I didn't even notice I was scratching, but you're right. My stomach has been itchy lately."

Tegan cut a glance at the now-empty bottle. She'd have to get some more, but she didn't know where or how.

"So, how are you enjoying life with the bounty hunter babes?" Max asked as she slid off the table, putting a hand on the woman's arm before she could answer. "Just so you know, I wasn't one of the original crew. Danica, Tori, Caro, Bexli, and Holly were the bounty hunter babes before they took me prisoner and before we all crashed on the Dothvek planet."

Tegan's mouth dropped open. "You're a prisoner?"

Max threw her head back and laughed. "Not anymore, but I used to have a price on my head, and they were the ones who found me."

Tegan looked at the woman skeptically. She'd always imagined bounties to be hardened criminals or outlaws. Not petite, female scientists.

"My discovery of an alternative fuel source had everyone after me. I was lucky Danica and her crew got me instead of the Gorglik named Mourad. He was terrifying, and he was the one who marooned all of us on the sand planet where the Dothveks live." Max winked at her. "Of course, that didn't turn out to be such a bad thing since the Dothveks saved us and helped us defeat Mourad."

Tegan slid her gaze to the woman's belly. "It seems like they did more than that."

Max's cheeks flushed. "Do you blame all of us for falling for them? They're huge, gorgeous, and brave."

"And they stuck around. That's not something I saw a lot of where I'm from."

Max cocked her head. "You're from that outpost on Zeroen?"

Tegan pressed her lips together as she nodded, thoughts of her home making her back stiffen.

"Is that where you learned everything about babies and childbirth?"

"My mother taught me. She said in a place like Zeroen, where the women are foolish enough to believe the men who never stay, it was a good job to have. We were always busy."

"That sounds hard." Max's voice was soft. "But not all guys run off. Just look at all the Dothveks on this ship. They might look tough, but when it comes to babies, they're marshmallows."

Tegan didn't know what a marshmallow was, but she'd seen the Dothvek fathers with their babies, and had to admit that they were besotted. From her experience, these alien males were the exception, and not the rule. She'd seen pregnant women abandoned too many times to believe anything else. It was why she'd promised herself that she'd never be stupid enough to lie with a man and why she never wanted a baby or family for herself. It was fine for others—and she could even find it in herself to be happy for them—but there was no way she was risking the heartache of being left behind and the difficulty of being a single mother. She'd seen her own mother struggle, working herself to the bone and into an early grave. That would not be her fate.

Tegan was aware that Max was staring at her. She cleared her throat, looked away quickly, and snatched up the empty oil bottle. She didn't know Max well enough to unload her dark thoughts about men, and it probably wouldn't be good for any pregnant mother's mental wellbeing to realize that their own midwife didn't believe in happily ever after.

"Found you!" Tori popped her head into the room.

"Me or Tegan?" Max asked, looking from one to the other.

"The doc," Tori said, then held up a hand before Max could say anything. "The baby doc."

Even though she wasn't a doctor, Tori and most of the others on board had been calling her doc, and she'd given up correcting them.

"Me?" She glanced at Tori's stomach. "Is everything okay?"

Tori made a face. "Like I told you, you won't have to worry about me at all. I was stopping by to see if you needed anything. We're making an unscheduled stop."

"The fuel leak? Max asked, her brow furrowed.

Tori cursed under her breath. "Holly still doesn't know how it happened. She and Rixx fixed the leak, but we won't be able to make it much further without refueling. Unfortunately, the nearest stop is Kurril."

Max's jaw dropped. "Kurril? As in, the place where you and Vrax almost died?"

Tori's already stern face darkened. "Trust me, if there was any place closer, I would not return to the Den of Thieves, but we can't afford to be dead in the water."

"Didn't you and Vrax leave under bad circumstances?" Max asked.

"You mean in the midst of ships exploding?" Tori waved a hand in the air. "No one knew it was us, and we were gone before the dust settled."

None of this sounded reassuring to Tegan. She'd assumed there would be some risk being on a bounty-hunting ship, but she hadn't expected it so soon.

"So, do you need any supplies while we're there?" Tori turned her attention back to the midwife. "Kurril might be a cesspool, but if it's sold, you can find it there."

Tegan looked at the empty brown bottle and thought of the other medicinal oils and herbs in her cabinet that were running low. "I do need more supplies."

"Give me the names, and I'll have Rukken get them for you."

Tegan shook her head. "I need to get them myself. I must be able to smell them to ensure they're genuine. Too many vendors try to pass off fakes, and only a trained nose can tell the difference."

Tori scowled. "You did hear the part of the conversation where I said that I almost died on Kurril, right?" She gave the woman a brief once-over. "And I'm guessing I've killed more people than you have."

"Maybe you can wait on the supplies?" Max suggested.

Tegan shook her head. "Not if I want to do my job well and keep you—and your babies—safe."

Max's cheeks paled, and she exchanged a glance with Tori.

The Zevrian huffed out a breath. "Fine. But I'm going to be furious if I lose our midwife on Kurril. She wasn't easy to find, you know." Then she pivoted to Tegan. "I'll let you go, but you have to take armed guards with you."

Tegan had no problem with an armed escort. "Will it be you?"

Tori gave a brusque shake of her head. "There may still be those who recognize me in the Den of Thieves. Same goes for Vrax." Her lips twitched. "I'm sending you with Dothveks no one will know."

CHAPTER

FOUR

Zaandr stole a glance across the compact mess hall then quickly returned his gaze to Rixx. But it hadn't been fast enough.

Rixx craned his head over his shoulder to peer at Tegan sitting with the captain and her mate, K'alvek. "Is that her?"

Zaandr's face warmed, as he tried to shrug it off and appear unconcerned as he focused on the bowl of spicy stew in front of him. "Is that who?"

His friend narrowed his gaze and frowned, jamming his knife into a chunk of meat and pointing it across the room. "The new female on board. Who else?" Then he leaned closer. "She is quite attractive, isn't she?"

Zaandr hated that his much suaver friend had noticed Tegan—how could he not?—and that he had expressed interest. Again, no surprise there. There was hardly a female who did *not* interest his best friend. Even on the sand planet where females were limited, Rixx had managed to seduce more than his fair share.

He avoided answering, glad that the chatter in the room

made his silence less noticeable. Not that his friend was focused on him. Not with a new female to draw his attention.

Zaandr inhaled the savory scents permeating the room as the crew ate the evening meal together, and felt a pang of homesickness for the Dothvek village. If they were on their homeward, they would be sitting around a crackling fire with the smell of burning wood and sizzling meat making their stomachs growl. As much as he had wanted to journey off his planet, a part of him would never feel that the steel beast of a ship was home.

"We are lucky, don't you think?"

Zaandr looked at his friend, jerked away from his thoughts of the sand planet. "Why are we lucky?"

"We are the only two unattached Dothveks, and this is a spaceship." He swiveled his gaze around the steel walls of the low-ceilinged room. "There is little chance for her to meet any other males."

"You assume she wants a mate."

Rixx grinned confidently. "Who would not want a strong warrior like us?"

Zaandr should be grateful that his friend included him when they both knew that his success rate with females was dismal. He allowed himself to glance at Tegan, as she swirled a lock of her brown hair around one finger and talked intently with Danica while the ship's captain bounced her baby on her knee.

It made sense that the ship had procured a midwife to tend to the pregnant females, but Zaandr sensed that Tegan truly had no other motivation to join the crew than to do her job. Despite Rixx's hopes, it seemed to him that the human had no interest in any of the single Dothveks.

"Don't even think about it," Tori said as she stepped in front of Rixx and blocked his line of sight to Tegan. She braced her hands on her hips and jutted out one hip, making it even more difficult for them to see the new crew member.

"Think about what?" Rixx managed to look both innocent and guilty at the same time.

Tori rolled her eyes and then grinned, baring her spiked back teeth. "We brought the midwife on board to assist with all the pregnant women. We did not bring her on board for some horny Dothveks to distract or get knocked up."

"Knocked up?" Rixx frowned. "We would never hurt a—"

"It means pregnant. Don't even think of getting our midwife pregnant, got it?"

Rixx's smug smile faded as Tori gave him an intensely menacing look. "Got it."

The Zevrian's stance relaxed. "She isn't interested in a mate, anyway. It was one of her selling points."

Zaandr could sense that Rixx didn't believe that. Rixx didn't believe that any female was immune from his charms, but he wisely remained silent.

"If you two can promise to behave, I have a job for you." Tori slid her gaze between them. "A job off the ship."

This piqued both Dothveks' interest, and Rixx straightedged.

"We need to make a stop on Kurril for supplies. Tegan needs to stop up on her herbs and medicines, and you two will be her bodyguards."

"Kurril?" Since Zaandr had never ventured off his home world, any planet sounded exotic to him.

Vrax strode up and curled an arm around Tori's waist. "I have many good memories on Kurril."

She elbowed him hard in the ribs, but her lips quirked at the corners. "You would only remember the good parts."

"You should consider it a testament to how much I enjoyed your—"

Tori jabbed her elbow so hard into his stomach that he coughed out a breath and put his hands to his side.

"Ignore Vrax." Tori cut a severe look to her mate. "Kurril is not a place most enjoy."

Zaandr and Rixx exchanged a glance.

"Is this because of the fuel leak?" his friend asked.

"It is." Vrax kept his hands on his side as Tori pivoted away and joined two female crew members at a nearby metal table, one Zaandr recognized as the ship's pilot and another he knew was the Lycithian shape-shifter because of her distinctive lavender hair. "If there was a closer planet than Kurril, we would go there. And if I was not known on the outlaw planet, I would join you."

"You are known?" He remembered hearing of Vrax's adventures when he'd stowed away with Tori on another bounty hunter's ship, but so much had happened to all the Dothveks after meeting the women that the details eluded him.

Vrax threw one leg over the metal bench and sat next to Zaandr. "I hope the aliens we angered have left Kurril, but there is much to avoid in the Den of Thieves."

As his kinsman outlined all the dangers of the city, Zaandr snuck a glance at Tegan. The thought of anything bad happening to the beautiful human with the tentative smile made his gut twist into a knot.

No harm will come to you on my watch.

When she glanced at him with a curious and confused expression, he jerked my gaze away. It was impossible that she'd sensed his thoughts. Wasn't it?

CHAPTER
FIVE

Zaandr stood with Rixx at the top of the lowered ramp and surveyed the planet. Dust swirled up with the hot wind, making it hard to make out the city beyond the shipyard. He could see the shapes of stone buildings, but the spires and towers blended in with the murky sky.

As soon as Vrax had told him about Kurril and the city on the planet known as the Den of Thieves, Zaandr had been both fascinated and nervous. Part of the appeal of joining his Dothvek brothers on the bounty hunting ship was the opportunity to see other worlds, but he was realizing more and more just how unique his home world was, and how dangerous the universe could be. His home planet might have its share of sand creatures, but it contained no hot spots for criminals and murders like the one he was viewing.

"Did Vrax tell you where this market would be?" his best friend asked.

Zaandr nodded. "Generally, although he was being dragged to a slave market the last time he arrived, so his memories aren't clear."

Rixx laughed then shot him a wary look. *You are serious?*

It only took him a glance to know that Zaandr was not teasing him.

"Are you my guards?"

The female voice from behind prevented Rixx from asking any more questions, and they both turned.

"Tegan." Rixx beamed at her as the woman eyed us both with obvious reservation.

He'd been strictly instructed not to delve into the minds of the humans on board, but it didn't take empathic abilities to know that she wasn't sure about this mission. He didn't know if it was the destination itself, or the two Dothveks, or a bit of both, but she was nervous.

"You have nothing to worry about," Rixx said, clearly picking up on her mood, as well. "We've been given directions to the market. We'll be in and out before anyone knows we're there."

Tegan wore a strange assemblage of brown clothing—pants tucked into lace-up boots, then topped with a hooded shirt and a duster coat that hung open to reveal a leather cross-body bag. Everything was worn and scuffed, but Zaandr thought she would probably fit in better than he and Rixx would with their bare, gold chests and tattooed arms.

Tegan flipped up her hood. "Then let's go."

She walked between them and down the ramp as both Dothveks walked briskly to keep up. Rixx caught her first, matching her stride as they walked across the dry, hardpacked ground and toward the stone arch leading into the Den of Thieves. Zaandr was half a pace behind, which he didn't mind, as he scanned the area around them for anyone approaching.

Even though Rixx was also supposed to be on his guard, he seemed more interested in talking with Tegan. That was fine by Zaandr. He wasn't good at talking to females, especially a pretty human. He remembered bumping into her in the corridor and their awkward conversation where he'd practically shouted at her that he wasn't the father of one of the babies due on board. He was sure the midwife thought he was crazy, or weird, or both.

At the moment, he couldn't worry about that. He was too busy taking in the approaching city and the low din of shouts and volatile chatter beyond the shipyard. But it wasn't the sounds of the city that concerned him, it was the swirl of dark thoughts and ill intent that hummed beneath the surface.

As they reached the imposing arch, Zaandr heard a high-pitched sound from below. He looked down and saw that Pog had followed them from the ship and was zooming around their feet. Tegan hadn't noticed, but Rixx was doing his best to hold her attention as he talked animatedly.

Zaandr scooped up the little green ball of fur. "You aren't supposed to be here."

Pog chirped at him then started purring. Zaandr shook his head and picked up his pace so that he was walking on the other side of the female.

"I think this is for you." He handed her the Lycithian creature.

Tegan stopped and stared down at the pet. "Pog! You aren't supposed to be here."

"I don't think he's a great listener," Zaandr deadpanned.

Tegan met his eyes and smiled. "I'm starting to think you're right." She sighed and stole a glance at their vessel across the shipyard. "I guess you're coming with us, naughty boy." She opened the flap of her crossbody bag, dropped him inside, and flipped the bag closed. "But don't make a fuss."

A tuft of green appeared at the corner of the bag, and Pog wiggled his head—at least Zaandr guessed it was his head—through the gap.

Zaandr stifled a laugh, and Tegan caught him, grinning along with him. Zaandr felt a jolt of warmth for the woman, that spread along his bare skin like sand sparks after a lightning storm.

"Like I was saying," Rixx raised his voice and resumed his conversation, but Zaandr tuned him out.

What had just happened? Zaandr's heart was beating fast, and his throat was tight. He clamped down any thoughts he might have, shielding them from his best friend. Luckily, Rixx was too consumed with himself to notice Zaandr's emotional flux.

That was all it was, Zaandr told himself. A momentary burst of irrational emotion. Because it was irrational to think that a female like Tegan would ever be interested in him. Despite his physical might and skills in battle, he was not good at interacting with females. Whatever charm had been in the family had clearly been taken by Vrax, who must have used his skills to win over his challenging Zevrian mate.

Zaandr had none of the ease that the other Dothveks had around females. He didn't even have the strong and silent energy that the elder Tommel—Bexli's mate—exuded. He was just nervous and awkward.

But not then, he thought. He hadn't felt nervous when he'd handed Pog to Tegan. He'd been able to smile at her and even share a joke. Something about the new midwife put him at ease. Something about her was both exhilarating and familiar.

As they walked under the massive stone arch and entered the city, Zaandr tried to focus on his task and ignore the fact that his best friend was openly pursuing Tegan. At least one of them needed to pay attention to the teeming crowds of unseemly characters milling about.

Their threesome gained a few curious glances, mostly directed at their gold skin and exposed chests, but none were malicious. It wasn't like they were the only aliens on the planet. He spotted creatures with various colored skin, some with shimmering scales, and even a few with tusks. Zaandr sent his mind into the crowd to sense for potential threats, and he was almost overwhelmed by the torrent of dark thoughts that flooded his mind. Vrax had warned him about the Den of Thieves, but he hadn't told him enough.

Zaandr stepped closer to Tegan as he picked up on pulses of desire from nearby males. Even though she was dressed like a male and had almost every part of her body covered, there were still those who wondered what was beneath her hood and all her layers.

A low growl tickled the back of his throat. An irrational desire to rip out the throat of whomever was thinking about Tegan startled him. Despite his skill as a hunter and fighter, Zaandr had never wanted to kill someone as much in his life.

You are not here to start a war. You are here to keep her safe.

He pushed aside his murderous instincts, remembering Vrax's instructions and guiding them through the crowds and down a series of passageways until they reached an open-air market. Faded fabric canopies sagged over stalls hawking everything from live animals, to books purported to contain magic. Bolts of fabric were unfurled, and baskets of strange produce overflowed.

The sounds of animals squawking and braying jostled with the noise of shopkeepers haggling over prices. The pungent scent of livestock mixed with the aroma of herbs and the sharp bite of the tanning shops, the combination on assault on his nose. It took all Zaandr's concentration to drown out all the actual sounds and smells so he could listen for dark intent.

"I'm looking for someone who sells medicinal herbs and oils," Tegan told then as she peered around.

Rixx walked ahead with his arms wide and one hand on

the curved blade hanging from his waist, parting the way for Tegan to follow.

"Your friend is wasting his time," she said, cutting her gaze to Zaandr.

He almost wasn't sure she'd spoken. "Wasting his time? Looking for your supplies?"

"No." She gave me a pointed look. "Trying to seduce me. It won't work."

Zaandr started to defend his friend and say that he wasn't trying to seduce her, but that would be a lie.

"It's nothing personal," she continued. "I'm just not interested in guys."

He blinked at her. "You prefer females?"

She grinned. "Not romantically. It's just that I don't want to take a mate, get married, have kids, any of those things I'm sure your friend wants."

"And you want none of those?" Zaandr had never heard of a female who did not want a mate. Or a male, for that matter. Unless she was a priestess, which Tegan was not.

She shook her head as she paused at a stall where bunches of herbs hung from the edge of the canopy. "I never knew my dad. Most of the women back home were single moms. From my experience, men leave. I don't want to be left."

Zaandr could sense her pain as if it were his own, a sad ache that twisted his heart and made him feel hollowed out. He put a hand to his heart, the words barely able to escape from his lips. "Not all males leave. A Dothvek would never leave his mate or child." The pain around his heart eased, and he was able to speak more forcefully. "Dothveks do not leave."

Tegan tilted her head. "Really? Then where is your friend?"

Zaandr spun around, his gaze searching for Rixx. Then he extended his mind to search for his friend. Nothing. He was gone.

CHAPTER
SIX

Tegan gave the Dothvek a knowing look as he swiveled his head wildly in both directions.

"He is gone," he said, his voice grave.

His tone startled her. She assumed his friend had wandered around the corner, but Zaandr was genuinely worried. "I'm sure he's not gone." She waved a hand at the stalls surrounding them. "He's probably scouting ahead."

Zaandr shook his head, and his long, dark hair swung around his face. "He isn't. I would sense that. I would hear him."

"Hear him?" Tegan readjusted her crossbody bag as Pog poked his head farther out.

"You do not know about Dothveks, do you?"

She was a bit taken aback. She knew what she'd seen— they were huge, gold-skinned warriors with ridges on their backs, and pointed ears hidden behind long, black hair. She also knew what Tori had told her, which, now that she thought about it, wasn't much. "I mean, I know you come from a sand planet, and Tori said this is the first time your people have left to explore space."

"That's true, but she did not tell you about our abilities?"

If this was going to be about their efficiency in getting females pregnant, she was going to kick him in the balls. She crossed her arms over her chest. "What abilities?"

He continued to glance around, his brow furrowed. "Our people can sense each other's thoughts and emotions. Occasionally we can sense those in other species, as well, but usually it is only between mates."

Tegan stared at him, suddenly self-conscious. "You can read people's minds?"

He frowned. "No. Not people. Dothveks. I can sense the emotions of my fellow Dothveks and communicate with them through our minds, but I cannot read minds."

Tegan released a breath. Okay, that wasn't so bad. At least he couldn't read her mind. Almost as soon as the Dothvek had said that he was empathic, she'd had the most inappropriate thoughts about him. Even now, she had to fight the urge to gape at the swell of his chest muscles, his corded stomach, and the intricate markings around his forearms.

Get a hold of yourself, girl. He isn't that *hot.* But that was a lie, and if he could read her mind, he'd know that, too.

"Maybe your friend got bored or found someone better to flirt with," she suggested, trying to lighten the mood. He had to be nearby. He couldn't have vanished.

"Rixx did not get bored," Zaandr snapped. "He would not abandon his mission, but he is gone. I can no longer hear him or sense him, and I am reaching my thoughts far."

"Gone?" Her nerves jangled. Suddenly, the market seemed more crowded and the cries of the street vendors more insistent. "He's a big, tough Dothvek. How could he be here one moment and gone the next?"

Zaandr scowled but didn't answer. He looked as confused and frustrated as she was. She could see how upset the alien was and how convinced he was that his friend hadn't left them on purpose. "I'm sorry I suggested that Rixx got bored or found another female to hit on. I was trying to cut the tension, but it was a dumb thing to say."

Zaandr shrugged one shoulder. "Do not feel bad. You do not know Rixx." He met her gaze for a beat. "And he was doing his best to charm you."

"And I'm afraid I wasn't very receptive, which is why I thought maybe he'd found someone who would appreciate his flirting, but you're right." She glanced around the market, noticing some sketchy characters eyeing them. "He wouldn't leave us like this."

"He vowed to keep you safe. We both did." Zaandr moved closer to Tegan, slipping an arm around her waist. "Stay close to me."

The warmth of his body flush to hers making her feel both more secure and more unnerved, but she didn't move away. Pog made a chirping sound as her bag bumped the Dothvek's leg. She reached across and ruffled the Lycithian creature's head. "It's okay, buddy. We'll be fine." She wasn't sure she believed it, but saying the words gave her comfort.

The Dothvek glanced at her, one slanted eyebrow lifting. Tegan had the strangest sensation that he could tell she was lying, but he'd told her that he could only sense the feelings of other Dothveks or a mate, and she wasn't either of those.

Pog wiggled again, working himself up until he popped from the bag and onto the ground. Tegan yelped as he hit the dusty paving stones and rolled.

"Pog! Where are you going?" She lunged for him, but he scampered just out of reach. "Come back here, you little maniac. Bexli will kill me if I lose you."

But Pog didn't come back. He scurried to the spot where Rixx had last been in view and snuffled on the ground.

Tegan blew out an impatient breath and reached for him again, but Zaandr grabbed her arm and held her back. "Wait. I think he's scenting Rixx."

Tegan cocked her head as the little green creature moved briskly around feet and stacks of wooden crates, clearly sniffing as he went. "Glurkins can track?"

The Dothvek shrugged. "I know little about Lycithian pets, but I do know tracking, and that's what he's doing. Maybe he'll have better luck with smell than I did with thoughts."

They followed closely behind, as Pog hurried around the nearby stalls and elicited the occasional shriek of alarm as he sniffed someone's leg. After a while circling the same spot, he sat down and made a mournful sound.

Tegan glanced at Zaandr. "What does that mean?"

The Dothvek's chin dropped. "He lost the scent."

She bent down and patted Pog's head before hoisting him back into her bag. "That's okay, buddy. You tried your best." She pivoted to Zaandr. "What do we do now? Do we continue to search for him or go back to the ship?"

"It would be wise for us to return to the ship."

"But you don't want to," she said, her instinct telling her that he was only saying they should go back for her benefit.

He frowned. "It doesn't matter what I want. I was tasked with protecting you. Now that Rixx has disappeared, I can no longer guarantee your safety."

"Do you think I'm in danger, or do you think since one Dothvek has vanished, you might be in danger of disappearing too?" The second possibility had just occurred to her, but as soon as the words left her lips, she knew they were right. She swiveled her gaze to the people who inhabited the place known as the Den of Thieves. They wouldn't care about a well-covered, nondescript human female in a place like Kurril, but burly, half-naked aliens with gold skin and ridged backs were a different matter. She knew that there were fighting competitions on the planet and slave auctions, and in both, a Dothvek would be a prize.

She slipped one of her arms around Zaandr's waist. "Maybe you're the one who should stick close to me."

He grunted as he started to move her in the direction they'd come. "If I am a target, then being with me puts you in danger. I need to get you to safety before I can look for Rixx."

Tegan remembered the stories Tori had told her about being on Kuril, about how she'd tracked Vrax to a slave market and then to the particularly dangerous madam who'd bought him. And that had been before he'd entered the fighting rings. She stopped walking.

Zaandr jerked to a stop and narrowed his eyes at her. "What are you doing?"

"It's my fault your friend is missing. If I hadn't needed supplies, neither of you would have been here."

"It is not your fault for needing supplies." He cast a dark look around them. "The only ones to blame are the ones who are behind Rixx's disappearance."

"Either way, whoever managed to take a Dothvek without you noticing or him being able to send you some kind of mind signal must be pretty clever or pretty deadly. Which means we don't have time to waste taking me back to the ship. We need to find him now."

Zaandr shook his head. "Impossible. If I let you remain here and in danger, I'll be failing at my mission. Rixx would understand why I cannot risk you for him."

"The faster we start looking, the greater the chance we can find him or find someone who saw something." She stamped one foot on the ground. "I'm not going to be the reason you don't find your friend."

She locked her gaze on him, hoping he would see how serious she was and that she should not be challenged on this. But even as she stared at him, her heart pounded with traitorous desire.

Focus, Tegan. Now is not the time to get a ridiculous crush. You have to find Rixx, not think about how good he felt pressed close to your side.

His eyes flared dark as one eyebrow lifted. "So be it." Then sighed, bent down, and tossed her over one shoulder. "If you won't come willingly, I will have to take you back to the ship by force."

CHAPTER

SEVEN

The female wiggled on Zaandr's shoulder as she struggled to get down, and she slapped one hand on his back as he made his way back through the bustling market. She used her other hand to keep her bag from falling and to keep Pog inside it. "Let me down!"

He ignored her cries, which were luckily drowned out by the frenzy of the vendors shouting about their prices and the animals screeching in protest from inside cages. The sight of a male carrying someone over his shoulder—even a someone who was clearly being taken against their will—didn't draw many glances. The lack of concern for the screaming female worked to his advantage, but it made unease tickle the nape of his neck. He'd been warned by Vrax that the Den of Thieves was treacherous, but Zaandr wondered what kind of place this was to allow such a thing to happen.

The kind of place where a Dothvek warrior could vanish without a trace, he thought darkly, his thoughts returning to his best friend, who was now missing.

Zaandr knew he had to move fast—get Tegan to the ship,

tell the other Dothveks, and mount a rescue. But where would they begin? They could start in the market where Rixx had last been seen, but he knew that the chances he was still there were slim.

Vrax had warned him about the Den of Thieves and told him about his own experiences and narrow escape. In a place that contained a slave market, more pleasure houses than he could imagine, fighting rings, and an underground market for all kinds of dark deeds, there was no doubt in his mind that Rixx had been taken for a reason.

He swallowed the sharp taste of bile that teased the back of his throat. He probably didn't want to know the reason.

Zaandr had known something was wrong from the moment he'd realized Rixx wasn't nearby and had reached out his mind—and sensed nothing. He wasn't used to nothing. On the bounty hunting ship, there were enough Dothvek minds to have a steady mental patter. Not to mention the females, who were not shy about conversation.

On his home world, he'd been surrounded by other Dothveks in his oasis village. There had been a constant buzz of thoughts and ever-present pulses of emotions. The only time he'd heard and felt nothing had been when he'd ventured onto the sands alone to hunt, but that had been rare. Usually, Rixx had joined him.

If there was any Dothvek he was accustomed to hearing constantly, whether at home or on the ship, it was his best friend. And now, there was silence.

"I know you can hear me, Zaandr." Tegan beat her fists on his back. "You might not be able to hear my thoughts, but you can hear my screaming."

He clenched his jaw. That was part of the problem. He shouldn't be able to hear her thoughts or sense her emotions, but he could. He'd picked up on that fact that she'd lied to Pog when she'd told him everything would be fine. She didn't believe that. She was as worried as he was. He could feel her fear and anxiety pulsing into him in waves, and it wasn't only because she was angry that he was returning her to the ship on his back. She'd been nervous before that. It had been her fear that had convinced him he had to return her to the ship.

Zaandr couldn't hunt for Rixx if he was being bombarded by the female's emotions. Not only was it distracting, but he also didn't know why it was happening. Tegan had made it very clear that the last thing she wanted was to get involved with him or any male. She clearly had strong feelings about fathers who left, and her answer to that was never to become a mother. Obviously, the best way to ensure that didn't happen was to avoid males altogether, which seemed to be her plan.

Not that he would have had a chance with a female like her, he reminded himself. She might not have welcomed Rixx's flirting but that was only because she rejected the idea of all males. If she'd been open to the idea of a mate, Zaandr was certain she would have been charmed by Rixx's attention and never noticed him.

Focus, he ordered himself, as he ducked down a corridor he was sure was the way they'd come.

It didn't matter if she was interested in males or mates or any of it. All that mattered was finding Rixx before something terrible happened to him.

"Zaandr!" Tegan yelled, her voice finally clear as they continued down the narrow corridor buffeted by high buildings, and there were no crowds to muffle her screams. "You have to let me down. You're going the wrong way."

He readjusted his hold on her legs, snorting derisively at her weak attempt to get him to release her. Then he looked at the passageway that was narrower and dimmer than any he remembered. The inset doorways looked dingy, and it smelled of fetid water. Was this the way they'd come?

His heart sank. He'd been so distracted by his thoughts about her and her thoughts that he hadn't paid enough attention to where he was going. He scowled and spun round. How far off track had he gotten? When had the corridor bent? He didn't remember turning, but now he couldn't see the crowds that had surrounded them only moments earlier. At least, it felt like moments.

Panic welled inside him. Rixx was gone, and now he and the female he'd sworn to protect were lost in the most dangerous city he'd ever entered.

"It's okay." Tegan's voice was calm and soothing. "We'll figure this out. Let me down, and let me help."

His shoulders slumped. He didn't know if she sensed his frustration, but she was right. He couldn't do this alone. Before he could swing her down to the ground, the hairs on the back of his neck prickled. Although he'd sensed danger since emerging from the ship and had tried not to focus on the dark thoughts and malicious intent of the crowds, this was different. This was near.

"You heard the lady," a voice said from the shadows. "Let her down."

CHAPTER

EIGHT

Her blood chilled when she heard the voice. It wasn't the hard, craggy voice of a man or really of anyone that belonged in the Den of Thieves. It was the sultry voice of a siren, beckoning them to do her bidding. But Tegan instinctively knew that obeying her would be the worst thing they could do.

Still, Zaandr lowered her to the dusty paving stones without a word. She shifted her crossbody bag so that it was behind her, giving a reassuring pat to Pog and feeling better when she could feel the lump she knew was him. At least she hadn't lost Bexli's pet.

"What are you doing?" Tegan whispered to him. She couldn't see whoever had spoken to then, but she could feel the female watching, so she hung close to him.

"You asked to be put down."

Now you start listening to me? Tegan wanted to snap, but it didn't seem like a good time to have an argument.

"I can't fight effectively with you over my shoulder," he added in such a low voice she almost thought she imagined it.

Her heart raced. So, he thought he would need to fight. That wasn't exactly what she wanted to hear, but at least she knew that he wasn't being fooled by the woman's sultry voice. At least he wasn't being lured by the female. For some reason, that thought sent a flush of possessive heat through her.

Zaandr cut a glance to her, his lips quirking to one side. Was he amused? Had he heard her? Tegan shook her head. Impossible. She wasn't Dothvek or his mate, and according to him those were the only minds he could read.

He cleared his throat and turned away, peering into the shadows of the corridor. "What do you want?"

"Why do you think I want anything?" she purred.

"I do not think it. I know it," the Dothvek said. "I can sense it."

Tegan joined him in searching the dark corners and recessed doorways for the owner of the voice. Where was she?

There was a high, tinkling laugh that was almost like child-like. "Maybe I do want something, but what if I told you it wasn't what you thought?"

"How do you know what we think?" Tegan asked, wishing her voice wasn't trembling.

"That's my secret." She laughed again. "I promise I wish you no ill will. I can help you find who you're looking for."

Zaandr drew in a quick breath, betraying his shock at her words. "How do you know we're looking for someone?"

"We aren't going to get very far if you continue to ask me the same questions."

Tegan shot a sideways glance at the Dothvek. Either this woman had seen Rixx being taken, or she'd been a part of it. Or, she thought with a gulp, she was some kind of witch. Tori had mentioned that the madam who'd held Vrax had been a witch with supernatural powers. Was this another of those? A shiver went through her as she wondered if the Den of Thieves was crawling with witches.

Zaandr's face was screwed up in a look of extreme concentration. Either he was having a stroke, or he was attempting to use his abilities to read her mind. Tegan still couldn't see who was talking to them, and the passageway appeared to be getting darker.

She peered overhead. Daylight was fading fast, and dusk was overtaking them. Soon, it would be dark, and they'd be lost in a treacherous city. They needed to forget about this mystery woman and run before it was too late. Before Tegan could whisper those thoughts to Zaandr, his face went slack.

He squared his shoulders and turned slightly. "We accept your help."

Tegan spun toward him. "We do?"

"She means us no harm."

"Says her," Tegan said under her breath. "How do we know she's not involved with the ones who took your friend? This could all be part of an evil plot to get *two* Dothveks. Maybe she wants a pair."

"Your girl has quite the colorful imagination."

"She's not—" Zaandr started to say, but Tegan cut him off with her own indignant outrage.

"I'm not his girl." She practically spit out the words. "I'm not anyone's girl!"

The woman emerged from the darkness, but Tegan would have sworn there had been nothing in the spot from which she stepped. Her dove-gray dress fluttered around her ankles as she walked, covered by a heavier cloak in the same color. "As you wish."

She walked past them, long, pale-blue tentacles flowing from her head like a mane of hair and swaying down her back. Her eyes were colorless, with no iris or pupil, but she looked at first one of them and then the other as she passed. "If you wish to see your friend again, I suggest you follow me."

Zaandr locked eyes with Tegan, but before she could tell him that this was a very bad idea, one phrase pulsed through her head. *Trust me.*

She was so stunned to hear his voice in her head that she didn't utter a word, as he took her hand and led her with him behind the unknown woman and farther into the Den of Thieves.

CHAPTER

NINE

Z aandr's mind roiled as he clasped Tegan's hand and walked behind the creature in gray. His instinct told him that the alien female would not harm them, but what if he was wrong? He hadn't sensed danger before Rixx disappeared. He hadn't even noticed his friend was gone before Tegan said something. Maybe his abilities were weakening the longer he was away from his home world.

Like all Dothveks, he'd always been taught that their planet held a certain power bestowed on it from the goddesses and that was what imbued them with the ability to sense thoughts and emotions. But his Dothvek brothers who'd left with the bounty hunters had not lost their abilities, even though they'd been far from the planet's pull for longer than he had. Even so, there had to be a reason he felt so muddled.

Tegan shifted her smaller hand in his. She was nervous and unsure of his decision to trust this stranger, but he didn't know if it was the expression on her face as she peered at him or his empathic abilities that told him this.

He squeezed her hand but didn't speak. How could he

explain that he didn't have a good reason for putting their lives in the hands of someone completely unknown? His only reason was his gut instinct and the sense that she wasn't dangerous. At least, not to them.

The female paused at an arch that led down a low passageway with almost no light and a heavy, loamy scent. She reached a hand into her cloak, produced two more gray cloaks, and handed them to the pair. "Put these on."

Zaandr eyed her, not sure if she was a spellcaster or just well-prepared. He took the cloak and shrugged it over his shoulders, watching as Tegan wrapped herself in hers and flipped up her hood. He did the same, trying to suppress the desire to snatch her up and run as far and as fast as he could.

"You okay?" she whispered, as they proceeded down the dank corridor, and the stone close on both sides brushed their shoulders.

He grunted for an answer, his senses on high alert as he picked up the frenzied chatter and energy of a large group. Since they'd left the marketplace, the assault on his brain had calmed, but now he gritted his teeth as he filtered out the cacophony of thoughts barraging him.

They approached a pair of short, but burly, albino creatures holding spears at their sides. The pair nodded at the female and stepped aside, revealing a door with faded, red paint and a tarnished, brass handle.

"Do not speak to anyone," the female warned them before flicking the door open and proceeding inside.

They followed her into a massive, multi-floor space with balconies ringing a central hall. The scent of earth was gone, replaced by the heady aroma of liquor and perfume with a faint undercurrent of sweat.

It was instantly clear to Zaandr that this was why he was being assaulted by so many thoughts. The place was packed with aliens of all varieties. Pink-skinned females were swinging on circular trapezes high above them as males hung from the balconies and cheered. Creatures with enormous eyes that never blinked danced around in swirling gowns and beckoned males to follow them, and slender males with delicate features paired off with burly males with beards. Couples slipped in and out of rooms, the desire and satisfaction rolling off them in waves.

"It's a brothel," Tegan said, her voice laced with disapproval.

Zaandr had only heard of such houses of pleasure, and the one Vrax had mentioned visiting while he was in the Den of Thieves had sounded much less raucous and more sinister.

The female leading them flicked a finger to urge them to stay close as she wound through the crowds. Many of the female entertainers nodded to her or waved, but she continued moving quickly. As they snaked through the gyrating bodies, Zaandr sensed curious gazes sliding toward him. They wondered who he was and why he was with *her*—not Tegan, but the female who'd found them. His face warmed as he picked up more thoughts about him. His head snapped up as he heard them wonder what was under his cloak and imagine all the things they would like to do to a male as large as him.

Zaandr strengthened the blocks in his mind and pushed aside the throbbing desire that surrounded him. He needed to focus on finding Rixx and keeping Tegan safe. Luckily, most of the patrons of the brothel hadn't noticed her, since her cloak didn't expose the lower half of her body.

After spiraling down a staircase that seemed to go on for longer than a typical flight of stairs, they were pulled through a door tucked beneath it. Once the door was shut, the music and voices were muted, and Zaandr allowed himself to take a deep breath.

Despite the atmosphere outside the door, the room was cozy. A fire crackled in a hearth and a high bed was topped with a neat, floral blanket. Two chairs and a low table huddled in front of the fire, and heavy curtains covered the only window. Instead of reeking of bodies and the perfume meant to cover the smell, this room carried the scent of burning wood and fresh linens.

Zaandr turned to ask their guide why she'd brought them to a brothel, but she slipped from the room and clicked a lock in place.

"What the hell?" Tegan raced to the door, yanking on the handle that held fast. Then she spun on Zaandr. "I thought you said to trust you about her."

So, she *had* heard him. The pleasure that this news brought him was dampened by the look of pure fury she was giving him. "I sensed no deception from her. I still don't."

Tegan fluttered her hand in front of the door. "Then why are we locked in?"

The door swung open, almost smacking Tegan, and she stumbled back as another female entered the room. This woman appeared human, with short, alabaster hair and green eyes that flashed as she took in them both. She definitely wasn't one of the entertainers, in her black, form-fitting, masculine clothing and matching thick boots. If Zaandr had to guess, he'd say she was a burglar, or thief of some kind.

"Apologies," the woman said, but it was clear that she didn't often apologize and wasn't all that sorry, as she braced her hands on her hips and stared them down. "But the Den of Thieves' only underground liberation movement can't be too careful."

CHAPTER
TEN

"Say what?" Tegan gaped at the woman. If the creature had sprouted extra arms, she wouldn't have been more surprised than she had by what she'd just told them.

The woman with white hair smiled. Her face was unlined, but her skin was tan, making the color of her hair even more striking. "You didn't expect to meet the leader of Kurril's underground?"

"Not in a whore-house," Tegan said, still not completely convinced this wasn't all a big joke.

The woman's brows lifted. "A pleasure house is the perfect place to keep a pulse on the darkness of the city, and lure unwitting informants." Her smile widened. "Besides, who would ever suspect a madam of running an operation to uncover criminals and liberate their victims?"

"Not me," Tegan mumbled.

"Is that what you do?" Zaandr asked. He didn't seem to be thrown be the revelation, although Tegan suspected that was because he was able to read minds. He must have known what was going on the entire time.

The woman nodded and shifted her weight from one leg to the other. "You can call me Rose. My associate who brought you to me is Astromeria. Meri for short. All the members of our organization are women, and we're all survivors of Kurril's seedy underworld."

"Those aren't your real names, are they?" Tegan asked. What were the chances both women were named after flowers?

"No," Rose said. "But it's better this way."

Tegan didn't have any argument for that. She liked the idea of a bunch of women surviving a dark place like Kurril and naming themselves after beautiful flowers.

"We know we can't stop all of what goes on here," Rose continued, "and if we disrupt too much, we'll be hunted down and eliminated. The crime bosses don't like it when their dirty money dries up. So we rescue one victim at a time, make small changes to make life a bit harder for those who hurt others, and cause revenue streams to inexplicably dry up."

"Isn't that frustrating?" Tegan asked. "You never win, and the bad guys are always popping back up to do more damage."

"The most important thing is keeping the victims we do save safe, and we can't do that if we aren't around." Rose waved a hand at the door behind her. "All those entertainers you see out there were once slaves or prostitutes in the direst conditions. Now they're here."

Tegan folded her arms over her chest. "But aren't they still prostitutes?"

Rose shook her head. "Our pleasure house is not what it seems. The males all leave here satisfied and with a strong desire to return, but they could never tell you exactly what happened. They think they drank too much or smoked too much prillyweed, but they don't know that they drink a potion that convinces them they had the time of their life and leaves them with a profound feeling of satisfaction and happiness. More than they've ever experienced at an actual pleasure house."

"So, you *are* witches?" Tegan knew she'd sensed magic from the female who'd escorted them. Meri undoubtedly had mystical powers.

"Not in the way you might think, but there are those of us who have powers. We do not curse people or cast hexes though."

"Vrax met a witch when he was on Kurril," Zaandr said. "She *did* believe in hexes."

Rose's face darkened. "There is a great deal of black magic on Kurril. Some of the victims we save are from those houses."

"I get that you help victims here, but why are you helping us?" Tegan asked.

Rose crossed to the fire and held her hands to it. "Meri saw your friend being taken. She said it was as efficient an operation as she'd ever seen. It wasn't an abduction of opportunity." She flicked her gaze at Zaandr. "Although I would not be surprised if anyone on Kurril wished to get their hands on aliens like you. You would be prized in the fighting pits, as well as in some of the pleasure houses."

Zaandr made a low noise in the back of his throat. "Rixx is a brave Dothvek warrior. I will not let him be abused or broken by those who deserve nothing but slow, painful deaths."

It didn't take an empath so sense the rage radiating from him, and it made Tegan shiver.

"I couldn't agree more." Rose pivoted back to them, and shadows from the fire danced across the side of her face, making her cheekbones seem even sharper. "But they took your clansman for a reason. It was like they were waiting for him. Do you have any idea why?"

"They couldn't have been waiting for him," Tegan said

before Zaandr could speak. "He's never been to this planet, and we only arrived today. Rixx didn't even know he'd be coming to the market until he was assigned to come with me so I could restock my supplies."

Zaandr waited for Tegan to finish and then he drew in a breath. "But we are not the first Dothveks to be on Kurril, or be known in the Den of Thieves. Our kinsman Vrax was here before."

"The one who met the witch?"

He nodded to Rose. "He did not leave her on good terms. He also won in the fighting pits and left the planet in dramatic fashion. The ship we arrived on was taken from Kurril."

"Are we passengers on a stolen ship?" Tegan hissed at him.

He avoided her gaze, looking at Rose instead. "Our skin and markings are distinct enough that the enemies he made could have been on the lookout for him since his departure."

Rose gave him a single nod. "We have sent our spies to confirm our theory about where he's being held. By morning, we will know and can formulate a plan to retrieve him." She pinned them both with a serious gaze. "Until then, you both must stay hidden." She took long strides to the door. "You will be locked in for your safety, but I'll have food sent up. I will return for you in the morning."

Then she slipped from the room and clicked the door behind her.

Tegan released a breath, weariness from the day overtaking her. Then she looked at the single bed and then at the Dothvek, who was also staring at the bed with a look of surprise.

This was going to be awkward.

ELEVEN

Zaandr could feel Tegan's exhaustion wash over him as if it was his own. The stress of being new on the ship and adjusting to space flight as well as all her crew mates, was added to the worry about Rixx and her fear of the Den of Thieves. And now she was staring at the single bed, and her panic was almost choking him.

"You don't need to be afraid of me," he said, fighting the urge to reach out and put a comforting hand on her arm.

"I'm not afraid of you." The words tripped from her mouth, but they were untrue. She lifted her crossbody bag over her head and put it on one of the chairs beside the fire. Pog tumbled out, gave himself a shake, leapt down, and hurried to the fire. He purred loudly as he circled a few times and then plopped down in a ball in front of the fireplace.

At least one of them would get some sleep, Zaandr thought as he eyed the stiff looking chairs. "I know you are. I can feel your fear, but you don't need to fear me. I have no intention of doing to you what you think I will."

She sucked in air and glared at him. "You're reading my mind!"

"I'm not trying to, but it's almost impossible not to sense your emotions, Tegan." He softened his voice. "Have you always been so afraid of males?"

Her gaze darted to his then fell. "I'm not afraid of males exactly. It's just I've seen too much pain and suffering they've left behind. I know exactly what one night of fun on a bed like that leads to." She jerked a thumb toward the bed covered in a flowery spread. "It's not fun for the mother left behind and alone."

"I know you've seen a lot of pain and heartache. I can feel it." He took a tentative step closer to her. "I promise you that I am not like any of those males. I cannot imagine abandoning a mother or a child, and I would die before I would ever do anything to hurt you."

She raised her head and gave him a weak smile. "I know you wouldn't. I don't know how I know, but I do. I'm sorry I overreacted. It was instinct."

Zaandr returned her smile, but it was wary. "I know how you know."

"What?"

"You know that I wouldn't hurt you because you can sense it. You're picking up my emotions and thoughts just like I'm sensing yours."

Her pupils flared wide. "Is that how I heard you tell me to trust you in the alley?"

He nodded, his lips pressed together.

"But how is that possible? I'm not Dothvek."

"Neither are the females on our ship, but they can sense the emotions of their Dothvek mates."

Tegan furrowed her brow. "But that's because they're

mated. It's not like they can read everyone's thoughts, can they?"

The corners of his lips twitched as he wondered what thoughts the female might have that she didn't want her crew mates to know. "Not that I am aware of, no."

"Then how is this—" she gestured between them "—possible?"

Zaandr wanted to tell her he had no idea, and that it must be a strange glitch, but that would be a lie. He knew why he could feel her. He'd felt a connection to her since he'd first bumped into her on the ship. He couldn't explain it, but it had only been growing stronger the more time he'd been around her.

Tegan's sharp gaze shuttered. "It's not all you, and I know it's not your fault. I've felt a connection to you since we met."

"You have?" This stunned him. She'd been so clear that she had no interest in him or any male, that he'd assumed all the attraction was on his side.

She moved her head up and down reluctantly. "I've spent my entire life trying to make sure this never happens. I grew up surrounded by women. I work with women. I see the reminders of bad men in my life every day." She sighed. "It was all working fine—until you."

Should he apologize for that? He still didn't know what he'd done to provoke this reaction. From what he'd heard from the other Dothveks who'd taken human mates, it wasn't something they did. It had happened naturally, as if the goddesses ordained it.

"I don't have any plans to force myself on you," he said. "Feeling a connection doesn't mean we have to act on it." He swallowed hard as he said this, because he knew that rejecting one's fated mate would be torturous, and he was getting a gut feeling that Tegan was his—like it or not.

She raised her gaze to meet his, her eyes pleading. "That's the problem. I don't want to deny this. I like feeling connected to someone." She choked out a watery laugh. "Even if it's a virtual stranger. I've protected myself from getting attached to anything and anyone for so long, I'd forgotten how nice it is to feel connected. I don't want to lose this."

His throat tightened. He didn't know how to respond. Rixx was the one with the charming words, not him. So, instead of speaking, he slowly stepped toward her and wrapped her in his arms.

He expected her to stiffen or even push him away, but she didn't. She melted into his embrace, curling her own arms around his waist, and pressing her cheek against his chest, her soft breath feathering across his bare skin. Her contentment pulsed into him, and he almost swayed on the spot from the headiness of it. His eyes closed as he let himself become awash in her swirl of pleasure.

Then his eyes flew open as her sunny thoughts unfurled the first tendrils of red-hot desire, and she started to kiss her way up his chest.

TWELVE

Tegan wasn't thinking. If she'd been thinking clearly, she'd have reminded herself that men brought nothing but trouble—and babies. Lots of babies. Usually, the thought of babies and memories of the hundreds of childbirths she'd experienced were like being doused with freezing water, but not this time. With the Dothvek, everything was different.

Standing with his arms wrapped tightly around her and the warm, spicy scent of him enveloping her, Tegan's resolve shattered. She'd never felt as safe and protected in her life. She knew he would defend her with his life, but she also knew in the depths of her soul that he would safeguard her heart as if it were his own.

It wasn't only wishful thinking on her part—the kind that had gotten more women than she could count in trouble. She could feel his intentions as if he was announcing them with a bullhorn. He would never hurt her, and he would never leave her. Not unless he was dragged away kicking and screaming, and, even then, he would claw his way back to her.

The strength of his devotion almost made her knees wobble. She'd never imagined that a man could feel such a thing—and to feel it for her? She had done nothing but push him away, and he would still walk through fire for her. She wouldn't have believed it if she wasn't feeling it humming through her like an unspoken vow that sank into her bones and permeated the deepest, most secret parts of her.

Tegan's fingers buzzed as she splayed her hands over the hard muscles of his chest and allowed herself to drink it all in. Her defenses crumbled like a house made of sand as she savored the devotion, and her eyes burned when she realized that she wanted more. She needed more.

She slid her hands over his gold skin, surprised by how firm it was but also so soft. The desire to be fully connected to him slammed into her, and she kissed his bare chest.

She'd never kissed any man's bare skin before. She'd never kissed anything but her mother's papery cheek or the downy head of a baby. But somehow she knew just how to kiss him. Somehow, kissing this Dothvek she barely knew felt as natural as breathing.

His flesh was warm under her lips and not at all like she'd imagine a male would taste. There was nothing foul or rank about Zaandr, and he tasted as good as enticing and spicy as he smelled. The taste of his skin sent more hunger pounding through her, as she kissed her way toward his mouth.

Tegan reached up one hand and slid it through the back of his hair, as she tipped her head back. Zaandr's eyes were molten black as he tangled his hands in her hair and held her head in place.

"Tegan," he rasped, "what are you doing?"

"I want you." Her voice wobbled. "I want all of you."

His gaze was intense as he searched hers. "Do you know what you're saying? Do you know what this will mean?"

She knew it would feel incredible. If it felt a fraction as good as touching him did, she was in, and she didn't care what happened afterward.

"You must care." His deep voice was insistent as his gaze slid from her eyes to her mouth. "You must know that there will be no going back, no retreating once we are mind mates."

Mind mates. She'd never heard of that, but if it meant being even closer with Zaandr, then she wanted it. "I won't want to go back. I don't ever want to go back to emptiness and fear."

"You are not thinking," he insisted. "You are intoxicated with pleasure."

"Good. Thinking has gotten me nothing but loneliness." She nipped at his skin. "This is much better."

He bit his bottom lip as she felt his own hunger for her crash over them both, his last shred of resistance wavering as the muscles in the side of his jaw trembled. "Tegan," he managed to grit out. "I cannot resist you."

She bestowed a wicked grin on him as she yanked his head so that his lips were brushing hers. "I don't want you to resist me. I want you to take me."

His grip on her hair tightened, and he crashed his mouth to hers. As delicious as his skin had been, his mouth was even more intoxicating. Tegan moaned as he parted her lips, his tongue swirling with hers in a sensuous dance. He slid his hands down her body, gripping her hips and hoisting her up until she could hook her legs around his waist.

She was vaguely aware of him walking them to the bed as they kissed, but her entire body throbbed with desire, and her head swam from the torrent of his dominant thoughts melding with hers, making rational thought impossible. When her back sank into something soft, she groaned into his mouth and arched into him.

Zaandr finally tore his lips from hers, panting as he peered down at her. He was bracing his body above hers as she lay under him on the bed. Even though she could still feel his primal need, he held her gaze in question. He knew she'd never given herself to anyone before, and he was hesitating.

Tegan put her hands on both sides of his face as her chest heaved. "I want this. I want you." Then she nibbled the edge of her bottom lip. "I *need* you inside me."

He closed his eyes for a beat and shuddered. He wanted her as much as she wanted him. More, even. His primal hunger was like a drumbeat reverberating through both of them as he pulled wildly at her clothing and growled.

Tegan lifted her arms so he could wrench her shirt off and wiggled her hips when he yanked down her pants, not caring that their desire was so insistent and frenzied. When her clothes were discarded, she sat up and tugged frantically at the waistband of his pants until she jerked it down far enough to release his cock.

She sucked in a breath when she saw it. Thick, long, and with raised rings down the length of it, it jutted proudly from his body. Her mouth went dry at the sheer size of it, as she brushed her fingers across the crown and was met with silky slickness.

A tortured groan escaped from Zaandr's lips as his gaze tracked her fingers, then he looked up at her, his gaze hot and needy. He let his gaze travel down her naked body, his grasp on control tenuous as one word dominated his thoughts. *Mine.*

Tegan opened her legs, so he could drag one finger through her slickness as his eyes nearly rolled back in his head. She coiled one hand around the back of his neck, pulling his head down so that her lips teased the tip of his pointed ear. "Then take what's yours, Dothvek."

With a roar, he notched his cock at her opening and plunged into her with a single, hard stroke, taking her breath and filling her so that she was finally whole.

THIRTEEN

Zaandr clenched his teeth hard as he held himself inside Tegan, her tight heat squeezing his cock so hard he was afraid the pleasure might stop his heart. He caught her mouth with his, kissing her softly and muffling her moans. Her hips twitched as her body stretched to take all of him, but despite the overwhelming urge to move, he held himself until her urgent movements stopped. The pounding need that had beat into him before had softened when he'd entered her, and now he felt the shock of her pain melt into pleasure.

He broke their kiss, touching his forehead to hers. "You are mine."

She made an unintelligible sound that he knew was her agreement. It didn't matter. Their fates were sealed, even if she did decide to fight him or run from him. She never could. Tegan was his. Their minds and bodies were one, and they would forever belong to each other.

Even as she opened her legs wider and arched her hips into

him, she didn't fully know what she was giving, but he would take it. He would take all of it as he claimed her as his.

Tegan curled her arms around his back, and her fingers traced the ridges along his spine before she reached his ass and dug her fingers into it.

He hissed out a groan. "You don't want it slow?"

She shook her head, her eyes wild.

"Tell me how you want me to fuck you," he ordered, his voice harder than it had ever been. Whatever shyness he'd had around females was gone. This wasn't just any female. This one was his.

"Hard," she whispered, as if the word was forbidden. "I want you to fuck me hard."

With a single, lightning-fast move, he snatched her arms and pinned them over her head. Her breasts quivered, the dusky nipples tight and pebbled, reminding him that there was so much more of her left to taste and to take. He held her hands down as he thrust hard inside her, savoring her throaty moans and how much pleasure he was giving her.

"Spread your legs wider for me," he commanded, frissons of euphoria humming through him when she obeyed him without question, his orders arousing her as much as him.

Now that she was open for him, Zaandr tilted his hips with each thrust so the vee of ridges leading from below his stomach to right above his cock could stroke her sweet little bundle of nerves. Tegan's husky cries made him move faster, his thrusts quickening along with the beating of his heart. His shoulder muscles strained as he ground his hips into hers, and she bucked against him. She didn't want to be released from his grip or his cock, but he thrilled at her feigned struggle.

"You can fight all you want," he growled, "but I'm going to fuck you until you scream my name."

Tegan arched her back so that he could catch one nipple in

his mouth. He sucked on the pebbly flesh and dragged even deeper sounds from her as ripples of pleasure started to slam into her and echo into him.

Zaandr released her nipple and her wrists, slipping his own hands down to clutch her hips. He leaned back and drove her onto him again and again. The sight of her stretched around his cock as she took every last bit of him sent a possessive thrill through Zaandr.

"You are mine, Tegan." He dragged his ridges across her sensitive bundle of nerves, letting himself feel the electric sensations barreling through her as he held his cock deep. Tegan grasped his hands as her body splintered, screaming as she spasmed around his cock.

Zaandr let the intensity of her release crash over him before he hammered into her fast and hard, throwing his head back as a blinding release tore through him like a blaze of fire. Heat scorched his skin and seared its way down his spine, as he poured himself into her.

He sank down onto the bed, pulling Tegan with him so that she was splayed across his chest, and he was still inside her as his chest rose and fell. He ran a hand down her back while she hitched in an uneven breath. "You didn't scream my name like I told you to."

"Zaandr," she whispered, his name sluggish as it escaped from her pleasure-addled lips.

He laughed. "Not what I meant, but there is always next time."

She let out a hum-sigh at this.

"There will be many next times now that you're mine." Claiming her had been even better than he'd imagined, and now he couldn't envision a life where he didn't spend every night feeling her come around his cock.

"I will need to be able to walk," she murmured. "You can't fuck me hard every night."

His heart leaped that she'd heard his deepest desires, and he curled both arms around her back. "Oh, with a body as perfect as yours, I can fuck you hard all day and night and never grow tired of you. But I don't mind carrying you."

CHAPTER
FOURTEEN

Tegan buried herself deeper underneath the covers. It was hard to get cozy on a spaceship, but the soft bed and warm blanket were making it easy to slip back to sleep.

Wait. She threw off the covers. She wasn't on the bounty hunting ship. The mattress on that bed wasn't nearly as soft, and there wasn't a crackling fire in her quarters.

She looked across the bed to where the fire still burned. Then she noticed a tray on the low table between the armchairs with a pot and two mugs along with a basket covered in a patterned cloth. Breathing in, she could detect the aroma of fresh bread.

The fire hadn't kept burning since the night before. Someone had entered the room and added more logs to it, and they'd left breakfast.

Tegan gulped and glanced over at the lump in bed beside her. So much for keeping what had happened between her and the Dothvek a secret. One advantage to hooking up in a busy brothel was that she hadn't worried anyone would hear them, but it seemed that was a moot point. She smiled when she saw that Pog had moved from his position curled up in front of the fire to the foot of the bed, and he was currently sleeping in a ball between their feet.

The delicious, yeasty aroma lured her from the warmth of the bed and even from the temptation of Zaandr naked under the blanket. He might have joked about carrying her around the ship after fucking her so hard she couldn't walk, but she did need to be able to walk today. Rescuing Rixx would take both of them fully functional.

She slipped quietly from the bed, careful not to disturb Zaandr or Pog, and found her clothes strewn across the wooden plank floor. She tugged them on haphazardly, not bothering to fully button the shirt or tuck it into her pants, and leaving the long coat hanging over the back of a chair. She also didn't bother with her underwear since she couldn't easily find it.

"Must be somewhere in the bed," she said under her breath as she tiptoed to the tray by the fire. She put a hand to the earthenware pot, almost sighing out loud from the warmth of it. She poured a cup of the hot beverage into one of the squat mugs and let the steam curl up from the dark surface as she unwrapped the cloth covering the basket and plucked a warm roll from inside.

Tegan bit into the brown crust and it crumbled in her mouth. She hadn't been expecting much from brothel food, but it was surprisingly good. The crust was crisp, and the insides were soft and yeasty, with an almost-sweet flavor. It was scads better than any bread she'd ever had at home, where good flour was expensive and butter almost impossible to find.

She polished off one roll, and then took a sip of the drink. Instead of it being watery and flavorless like the rationed, herbal teas she'd grown up on, it was rich and sweet with a bit of bite when she swallowed.

Walking to the fire as she sipped, Tegan already felt more hopeful about their situation. Yes, they were technically locked up in an alien whore-house, but she believed the leader of the resistance when she told them that they would find Rixx. She also knew that Zaandr would protect her, no matter what happened. There hadn't been much about her life so far that had been certain, and she liked the unusual sensation of having one thing that was. For her, the Dothvek was as solid as stone.

"How long have you been up?"

His gruff voice from the bed startled her, and she almost choked on her drink. She coughed and gave him an apologetic grin. "I didn't know you were awake." She glanced at the crumbs scattering the floor. "Did I wake you with my crunching?"

He sat up fully and cocked his head to one side as Pog roused himself from the end of the bed and gave a small shake of his green fur. "No, but I could sense how much you enjoyed it."

Her cheeks warmed as she plucked another roll from the basket. That's right. He could feel what she did, and much stronger than she could sense him, although it wasn't hard to pick up on early morning contentment or the faint buzz of his arousal.

She glanced down at her disheveled clothing and put a hand to her tousled hair. He couldn't be turned on by her now, could he?

"You should not doubt your appeal," he said with a grin. The covers had fallen to his waist, exposing his bare chest.

Tegan narrowed her eyes at him and gave him a smirk. "Right back at you."

Pog jumped from the bed and scampered over to her, running in circles around her feet until she scooped him up. He purred as he sniffed the warm roll in her hand.

Tegan laughed and rolled her eyes. She tore off a small bite and fed it to him. "You're a bit of a beggar, you know."

"I didn't have to beg last night," Zaandr said, as he searched the floor for his leather pants and boots.

Tegan snorted out a laugh as she gave the Lycithian creature another morsel of bread. "I wasn't talking to you. I was talking to the glurk...I was talking to Pog."

The Dothvek pulled on his pants, and Tegan averted her eyes as he tucked his significant package down one leg. Why did she suddenly feel shy? She hadn't been even remotely shy the night before. Thoughts of her lusty behavior made her pulse flutter. Nope. That had not been an issue.

In the light of day, she was shocked by her own lack of inhibitions and how quickly she'd discarded her conviction that she would never lie with a man. Technically, Zaandr wasn't a man, he was a Dothvek, so that part still held, but she hadn't been able to hold the line when it came to her sex embargo.

Another furtive glance at the muscular alien reminded her why. Had she really stood a chance against someone so beautiful and someone whose honorable thoughts she could feel as if they were her own? Knowing that he would never contemplate doing any of the things she feared a man would do had shattered her resistance and made surrendering to him and to a night of pleasure possible.

Despite all she'd seen in her life and how many times she'd sworn she would never fall for a handsome face and sweet words, Tegan didn't regret the night before. She didn't regret finally allowing herself some measure of joy, some pleasure.

She didn't regret any of it, even though she had to admit that their situation wasn't ideal.

Oddly, being in the dangerous alien city and hidden away in the brothel with Zaandr as they searched for his missing friend was the happiest she'd ever been. But a little voice in the back of her brain reminded her that happiness rarely lasted.

When he was dressed, she set Pog on one of the chairs, poured him a mug of the hot drink and held it out to him. "I'm not sure what it is, but it's good."

Zaandr took it and gave her a warm smile before sipping it. His eyes widened as he swallowed. "I didn't expect sweet."

"Do Dothveks not have sweet drinks in the mornings?"

He shook his head. "Sugar is rare on the sands." He took another sip as he snagged a roll from the basket. "But I like this." He took a bite of the bread, and closed his eyes for a beat. "I like this even more."

For a moment, the three of them ate and drank in companionable silence. Tegan couldn't help but smile. If you didn't know that they were locked in the room and that it was inside a brothel, they would have appeared like a happy little family. The thought warmed her heart and made tiny alarm bells go off in the deep recesses of her mind.

"Tegan?" His voice was gentle, but his eyes were probing as he looked at her.

Before she could respond, the door clicked and swung open. Rose stepped inside, flanked by a pair of equally impressive females. She eyed them both, flickered an eyebrow, then braced her hands on her hips. "Ready to go save your friend?"

CHAPTER

FIFTEEN

"We're ready." Zaandr shoved the last bite of the warm bread into his mouth and washed it down with the rich, sweet drink. He was anxious to find Rixx, although he wished he could have asked Tegan about the fear he felt within her. Was she worried about their mission today, or had their night together triggered something?

For him, last night had been the best of his life, and he had no doubt that he'd found his life mate. But humans didn't have the same tradition of mind mates or the fates of the goddesses bestowing on you one great love. Tegan had grown up with a different reality and no examples of happily mated couples.

When she'd fallen asleep in his arms, he'd had no doubt that she'd been happy. He could feel it enveloping him. But they were no longer in bed basking in the afterglow of their coupling, and reality was intruding and melting away their euphoric haze. Already, his mind was focusing on saving Rixx and keeping Tegan safe in the process.

"Like I told you last night, our operatives were searching

for your friend." Rose strode further into the room. "They confirmed that he's being held by a band of Zevrian mercenaries."

"Zevrians?" Tegan glanced at Zaandr, and a sick feeling churned in his gut.

"Does your friend have a history with the Zevrians?" Rose asked, swinging her head from one to the other.

"He does not," Zaandr said, "but we are not the first Dothveks to come to Kurril. My kinsman was in the Den of Thieves before and encountered some Zevrian mercenaries. He got the better of them."

Rose nodded solemnly, her brows pinched together. Then her gaze darted to the tribal markings around his forearms. "That would explain it. You are a distinctive species. If you were spotted in the market by one of the Zevrians, they might have mistaken your friend for your kinsman who wronged them."

Zaandr feared that the sweet bread and drink would rush back up. If the Zevrians through that it was Rixx who'd killed some of their crew mates and taken their ship, there was no telling what they were doing to his best friend right now. "We should go."

Rose nodded. "You should wear the cloaks that were given to you yesterday." She cast a quick glance to where they were folded across the back of a chair, then her gaze caught on Tegan's panties that had fallen to the floor when he'd pushed back the covers. Her lips twitched, but she said nothing. "Have you eaten enough?"

He nodded as Tegan grabbed her crossbody bag and slung it over one shoulder, then tucked Pog inside it.

"We're good," she said, snatching one of the cloaks from the chair and pulling it over her shoulder.

Zaandr did the same, stepping in line as Rose led them

from the room. He looked over his shoulder at the cozy room and wished they had more time there, but a part of him also twinged with guilt that they'd been warm and fed while Rixx had been held prisoner by Zevrian mercenaries for something he didn't do.

It was too much to hope that the Zevrians had realized their mistake and not punished Rixx for Vrax's actions. Even though he was not close enough to his fellow Dothvek to detect distinct emotions or thoughts, he was certain Rixx had not had a good night. He could feel it in his bones, as if his body was somehow absorbing the distant pulses from his best friend. The faster they reached him, the better.

Rose led them through the brothel, although now there were no girls swinging from hoops and no music blaring. The balconies were free from ladies hanging over and waving to patrons below, and the thick, wooden doors were all shut tight. The scent of stale liquor and perfume still hung heavy in the air, but it was like an echo of the raucous night before.

When they reached the exit, Rose flipped up her own hood and her nubby, brown cloak covered her almost entirely. The tough women with her did the same. Tegan twisted her head to meet his eyes and smiled at him before she followed their lead, and they all ducked through the door and into the dank, narrow passageway.

The Den of Thieves in the early morning was a very different place. Like the brothel, it seemed empty and unnervingly quiet. The warm sun barely slatted above the rooftops, the light still not reaching the dark labyrinth of corridors that made up the city. Their footsteps tapped on the worn paving stones as they hurried down one alley and then another.

Zaandr could tell they were skirting the center, but he was sure the resistance leader had a reason. Although Kurril was filled with creatures who didn't wish to be seen, their group might draw a few unwanted glances.

He kept his gaze focused on Tegan. She was both nervous and excited, normal emotions when you were about to stage a rescue. He'd wanted to suggest that she stay behind, but he knew that she would have rejected that and been offended that thought she couldn't take care of herself. He didn't think that, but the fact was, Tegan wasn't a trained fighter. She was a brilliant healer and midwife, but she would not be much use if they ended up fighting hand-to-hand. As much as he cared for Rixx, he would not sacrifice Tegan for him.

Not now. Not when he knew without a doubt that she was his. Not when he was tied to her as if their hearts were beating as one. He groaned as a primal need to protect her swelled in his chest. Would his desire to protect her distract him from the mission?

Rose stopped and they all hunched down behind her, as she bent low behind a stack of rickety crates. She nodded to a three-story, brown stone building with faded, black shutters closed tight over narrow windows. "That's it. That's where they have your guy."

Zaandr reached out his mind for Rixx. Now that the city was sleeping, it was easier to parse the mess of thoughts. He locked onto his friend's mind, almost gasping when he found him. "He's there, and he's alive."

The resistance fighters stared at him curiously.

"Dothveks can read minds," Tegan said.

"I'm coming for you, Rixx," Zaandr whispered, as much to himself as to his friend.

The single, urgent word that Rixx sent him made fear ice his flesh.

Hurry.

CHAPTER
SIXTEEN

Tegan felt Zaandr stiffen beside her, even though they weren't touching. Fear arrowed through him and into her, and she sucked in a sharp breath. "We need to hurry."

The resistance fighters looked from her to the Dothvek, whose face was set in a grimace, and they nodded grimly.

"We can't just rush in," Rose said.

"Why not?" Zaandr cut his gaze to the building. "The Zevrians are either asleep or passed out, so they won't put up much resistance if we go in fast and hard."

Rose studied him for a beat. "You really can read minds?"

"Not every mind, but I can communicate with my Dothvek brothers through our thoughts. Rixx is on the top floor in a front room with the windows covered."

"I couldn't sweet-talk you into staying on Kurril and fighting with us, could I?" The resistance leader asked, her voice teasing but her intent serious.

Zaandr raised his brows at her in answer.

"Never mind." She waved a hand in the air. "You're here

now." She pivoted back to face the building. "We have two more resistance fighters positioned in the back as lookouts, and in case the Zevrians try to run."

Tegan drew in a deep breath. She'd never been involved in a rescue mission before, or any fight, really. She didn't even have a weapon, although she wasn't cocky enough to think she could handle a blade like the curved one that hung from the Dothvek's waist.

"She needs a blaster," Zaandr said, clearly stealing into her mind and reading her worries.

One of the women slapped a battered weapon in her hand. "You ever shot one before?"

Tegan shook her head, trying to keep her hand from trembling.

"It's easy," the woman with wiry, black hair told her. "Point and squeeze."

Tegan gripped it, and the woman slid her finger off the trigger. "Only put your finger there when you're ready to shoot."

Tegan nodded and swallowed hard. She could do this. The Zevrians were all asleep anyway. She could hit a target that wasn't moving.

"Stay behind me," Zaandr whispered to her. "I'll clear the rooms. If I get in trouble, shoot." He glanced at her blaster. "But tell me to duck first."

She wasn't sure if going in behind him was better or worse. The last thing she wanted to do was shoot him.

"You won't," he said, locking eyes with her. "I trust you."

Tegan wasn't sure if his trust was fully warranted, but she was touched that he said that. It did calm her rattling heartbeat, as Rose waved for them to follow her.

They walked swiftly and silently across the small square fronting the building, but before they reached it, the door opened, and a Zevrian stepped out. Tegan knew it was a Zevrian because he had the same brown skin and bumps over his eyebrows and across his temples as Tori.

Rose stopped and turned, but Tegan had an idea. She kept walking but made her steps uneven as she threw back her hood.

"Excuse me," she drawled, intentionally slurring her words.

The Zevrian frowned as he looked up. He looked rough himself, with bloodshot eyes and clothes that looked slept in. "Yeah?"

"I'm looking for the market," Tegan said, rubbing her eyes as if she'd just woken. "But I think I'm lost."

The Zevrian snorted out a derisive laugh. "You sure are. The market isn't near here."

"No?" Tegan made a big show of turning in a circle as if looking for it. "Well, do you know where it is?"

The Zevrian walked toward her and away from the front door of the building. Now that he was closer, he focused on her, giving her a leering smile as he looked her up and down. "Why do you want to go to the market? Why don't you stay here with me?"

From the corner of her eye, Tegan saw the two resistance fighters slip into the building behind the Zevrian. Zaandr didn't go inside. He was sneaking up on the Zevrian.

"Here?" Tegan tried to sound as clueless as possible as she smiled at the Zevrian. Pog wiggled in her bag, but she put a hand on the leather flap to quiet him.

He jerked a thumb behind him. "In there. I can show you a better time than you'll have at the market. "He put a hand on her arm. "Besides, a pretty thing like you shouldn't be walking around the Den of Thieves alone."

"She's not alone," Zaandr said from behind.

The Zevrian whirled around, but he wasn't fast enough. Zaandr plunged his arched blade into the alien's gut before he could even scream. Holding the blade inside him, Zaandr maneuvered the alien into the alley beside the building and dropped him in the shadows, sliding his blade out and wiping the blood on the Zevrian's pants. He took the Zevrian's blaster and tucked it into the back of his pants.

He met Tegan's eyes, as she heaved in jerky breaths. "Good work." Then he motioned with his head to the door into which the female resistance fighters had disappeared. "Let's go."

She ran behind him as they entered the building. She'd seen people die before, but this was the first time she'd seen one killed up close. She knew why Zaandr had done it, and she knew he'd had no choice. Even so, it sent chills down her spine.

Tegan blinked as her eyes adjusted to the dimly lit front room, but she could make out one dead Zevrian slumped on the floor in the corner. Zaandr didn't pause, moving swiftly to the next room, which was empty. Sound of fighting came from the floors above, and Zaandr sped up, vaulting up a narrow staircase three steps at a time.

Tegan ran behind him, but there was no way her legs could keep pace with his significantly longer ones. When she reached the top of the stairs, she glanced around but didn't see him down either of the two hallways that extended to both sides. There were sounds of fighting and blasters firing from all directions now, and she didn't know where to turn.

Making a wild guess, she ran down one of the hallways, peering into the open doors. Dead Zevrians, but no Zaandr. She reached the end and spun around just as a Zevrian stepped in front of her. Blood trickled from his mouth as he swiped it away with the back of his hand. Tegan peered into the open doorway he'd just left, and her stomach lurched when she saw the resistance fighter who'd given her the blaster lying on the floor in a puddle of blood.

The Zevrian fixed his black eyes on her. "Looks like you're next."

Tegan fumbled for her blaster but was knocked to one side by a violent movement. When she righted herself, her leather bag was in tatters, and she was standing beside a hulking, green beast with scales and a long tail.

Terror arrowed through her until the creature slid his gaze to her, the eyes so familiar she gasped. "*Pog*?!"

CHAPTER
SEVENTEEN

Zaandr heaved in a breath. His blade dripped blood as he stood over the Zevrian he'd just dispatched. Rose stood behind the dead alien, her eyes wide and her blaster at her side.

"Thanks for the save," she said. "I didn't hear him sneak up on me."

Zaandr inclined his head to her. "That's two floors cleared. Rixx is on the third."

Rose furrowed her brow. "Where is your girl?"

Zaandr looked over his shoulder. He'd thought Tegan was right behind him when they'd been running up the stairs, but he hadn't checked when he'd raced down the hallway and seen Rose about to be ambushed. The intensity of the fighting had muddled his mind, and all he heard was the rushing of blood in his ears. Until he heard the roar.

"What was that?" Rose asked. "Are they keeping some sort of beast in here?"

Zaandr didn't hesitate. Now he could sense Tegan's fear, but also...surprise?

He retraced his steps, following the sound of the second roar down the opposite corridor and turning the corner just in time to see a burst of fire engulf a Zevrian warrior. The enemy combatant was instantly consumed by the flames and staggered into an open doorway flailing his arms and screeching.

Zaandr assumed a battle stance as he peered through the dissipating smoke, and he prepared himself for whatever beast had unleashed that fire. But his gaze went to Tegan, who stood calmly next to a green creature who had smoke curling from its mouth.

"It's Pog!" Tegan yelled. "He transformed and saved my life."

Zaandr shook his head. Had he heard her correctly? He squinted at the green beast. That was the tiny Lycithian glurkin? He knew that Bexli's pet was a shape-shifter, but he'd never witnessed him shift.

He carefully approached the beast, holding out a hand. The creature nuzzled him with his scaly head and purred. It *was* Pog.

Rose skidded up behind him. "Whoa. Where did that come from?"

"This is Pog," Tegan said, rubbing the creature's back. "He's a Lycithian shape-shifting pet, and he just saved my ass."

Rose blinked a few times. "Well done, Pog." Then she eyed Tegan and Zaandr. "You all continue to surprise me."

Zaandr was still processing the strange turn of events, but there was no time to dwell on the bizarre fact that tiny, fluffy Pog was now larger than him and covered in scales and spikes. "We still need to find Rixx."

Rose cast her gaze heavenward. "One more floor to search."

Zaandr knew his friend was on the top level, so he led the way as they all hurried down the corridor and up the tight staircase. They didn't encounter any more Zevrians, and Zaandr suspected they'd all rushed to the sound of the fight. He knew better than to count his sand hens before they were hatched, but he hoped that they'd encountered the last of the enemy.

Using Rixx's thoughts as a guide, he ran past the first few closed doors. His friend was in the room on the end that faced the front of the building, and he didn't even pause before hurling his foot into the wooden door.

The door flew in, splintering from the force of the blow. Inside, strapped to a chair, was Rixx. His face was bruised, and dried blood caked the side of his head, but he grinned when he saw them.

"It sounded like you were killing everyone in Kurril before coming upstairs," he said, meeting Zaandr's gaze. "Did you have all the fun without me?"

Zaandr shook his head, not surprised that his friend was still in good spirits. It would take more than a few mercenaries to subdue Rixx.

Rose and Tegan entered the room behind him, and Rixx's eyes widened. "I like this rescue party. I didn't think you had it in you, brother."

Zaandr rolled his eyes as he hurried forward to untie him. If Rixx tried to seduce his rescuers, he might decide to leave him tied up.

Rixx eyed him with a startled expression. "You wouldn't."

Try me, Zaandr told him.

His friend glanced at Tegan and then narrowed his gaze. *What have you been up to while I've been tortured?*

Zaandr peered at his friend's head wound, which superficial. *Tortured? You've looked worse after encountering a giant turtle on the sands.*

Rixx shook his hands after Zaandr untied him and touched his wrists where they'd been rubbed raw. *You're changing the subject.*

"You okay?" Rose asked, unaware that Zaandr and Rixx were carrying on a conversation without speaking.

"This is Rose," Zaandr told him. "She's the leader of an underground resistance in Kurril. She's the reason we found you."

Rixx's expression became serious. "I owe you a debt of gratitude."

"Saving you and eliminating some mercenary scum at the same time is all the thanks I need." Rose smiled at him. "But you're welcome. Now, I'm going to go back down and see if my fighters are okay."

She ran from the room, passing Pog and patting his side.

Rixx seemed to finally focus on the green, scaled creature in the room. "What in the—?"

"It's Pog," Tegan said before he could finish. "He shifted to save me."

Rixx rubbed his temple. "At least I'm not hallucinating."

Zaandr stepped closer to him. "Can you walk, or do you need help?"

"I can walk." He raised an eyebrow in challenge. "I can race you out of here, if you'd like."

Tegan sniffed and then frowned. "Do you smell that?"

Smoke. Zaandr's stomach clenched as he ran to the doorway and peered down the hall. Black smoke was billowing up from the floor below. The Zevrian who'd been on fire must have set other things alight as he'd been running and flailing.

"We can't get out that way," Tegan said in a small voice as she stood next to him.

Zaandr pressed his lips together. They were on the third

floor, and he'd seen no external stairs anchored to the outside of the building. His gut clenched into a hard knot of fear. What other way out was there?

EIGHTEEN

Tegan coughed and put a hand over her mouth and nose. The acrid smoke was rising fast, and she could see orange flames licking the top of the stairwell. There was no getting out through the building anymore.

"Back in the room." Zaandr pulled her inside and shut the door.

Rixx was already wrenching the boards from the window and tossing them behind him. Zaandr ran to help him, and the two Dothveks cleared the window in a matter of seconds. They tugged at the sill, but it was stuck, so they exchanged a knowing glance before both raising their boots and kicking out the glass.

She ran to the window and peered down. Rose was below them with both of her fighters, but they'd managed to avoid the cascading glass. The fighter she'd seen lying on the floor looked badly wounded, but she held a hand to her bloody side as she looked up at the burning building. Smoke now poured from the windows below them, sending a pillar of black into the sky.

"So much for an in-and-out mission," she muttered from behind her hand. People were already streaming from nearby buildings and gaping up.

"We have to jump," Rixx said.

·"From this high?" Tegan shook her head. "We'll never survive." Then she eyed the huge, muscular Dothveks. "Correction, *I'll* never survive."

Zaandr's face contorted in pain. "You can jump with me. I'll hold you."

She shook her head. "No way. I know what that means. You'll shield me and then the fall will kill you."

"It's my choice."

She folded her arms over her chest, the ache in her heart palpable. She would not be the reason he didn't survive. She wouldn't be able to live with that.

Her eyes burned, partly from the stinging smoke, and partly because she was furious with herself. This was exactly why she didn't want to get involved with anyone. They always ended up leaving, even if they promised they wouldn't. Even if they didn't want to be taken away.

"As much fun as it is to watch you two bicker like my parents," Rixx said, "we need to focus on escaping. There has to be another way down."

Tegan took a shallow breath and fought the urge to cough. Gray tendrils of smoke were curling long fingers under the door, and it wouldn't be long until they couldn't breathe at all.

Pog let out a stifled roar and gave himself a shake, the scales vanishing as he shrunk and sprouted green, feathery wings.

"Pog!" She threw her arms around his neck. "You're a genius!"

"You can fly us down?" Rixx ruffled the tuft of feathers on the bird's head.

Pog ambled to the window and climbed onto the sill. He craned his neck and motioned for Tegan to get on his back. That was a yes.

She climbed on, wrapping her arms around his neck for balance and making a point not to look down or think about her newly discovered fear of heights. She glanced back at Zaandr. "Now you get on behind me."

He shook his head, exchanging another glance with Rixx. "There isn't room. Pog won't be able to hold more than one of us and fly."

Pog made a chirpy sound that sounded like an agreement. The Dothveks were huge and almost all muscle, so the creature must know that he would drop like a stone if one climbed on with her.

Tegan started to slip from his back. "Then he can transform into a bigger bird."

Rixx shook his head. "Then he won't fit out of the window and the sill won't support him. We have to go one at a time."

Tegan's heart sank. She knew they were right, and that there was no time to argue. She needed Pog to fly her down so he could return for the others. But that didn't change the sick feeling roiling in her gut that told her this was not going to turn out well. She was not going to get her happily ever after with Zaandr, because life wasn't like that.

She hated that her mind went to the negative, but it was the way she'd protected herself for most of her life. Don't get attached. Don't get hurt. The pain in her heart told her it was too late for that. This was going to hurt bad.

Zaandr wrapped her in his arms and murmured in her ear. "I told you I would never let anything hurt you. That is a promise I mean to keep."

"But," her voice cracked.

"Do you trust me?" He pinned her with an intense gaze that made her breathe hitch in her throat.

Tegan bobbed her head up and down. *I do.*

He cupped her face with one hand. "We are going to survive this, and I'm going to spend the rest of my life making sure you get your happily ever after, if you'll let me."

Her throat tightened, as he pulled back and met her gaze. *I love you, Tegan.*

The shock of his unspoken words made her mouth open. She wanted to say it back to him or think it back to him, but the shock had stunned her into silence.

Zaandr backed up and slapped Pog on the rump. "Go!"

Without hesitation, Pog leapt from the window and unfurled his wings. Tegan was caught between wanting to grasp his neck to stay on him and needing to look back at the window and at Zaandr. Her heart pounded as they soared down through the air, circling the square below until they landed.

Tori rushed up to her, with Vrax close on her heels. "What the fuck? We've been searching for you everywhere!"

Tegan slid off Pog's back, her legs so shaky they almost buckled when she touched the ground. She met the bird's eyes. "Go get Zaandr and Rixx."

Pog took off into the air again and soared to the window, which was now emitting white smoke.

"Zaandr? Rixx?" Vrax followed the bird's flight. "They're inside the burning building?"

Rose came up to them and hooked an arm under Tegan's, seeming to know that she was about to collapse. "Rixx was being held by Zevrian mercenaries. We rescued him."

Tori's brown skin paled a few shades. "Zevrians?"

Rose flicked a quick glance over Tori, no doubt registering that she was also Zevrian. "They're all dead."

"Good." Tori turned her attention back to the building as Vrax muttered something in Dothvek.

Tegan's pulse quickened when she spotted Pog in the window with a Dothvek on his back, although she couldn't tell through the smoke which one. As much as she didn't wish Rixx harm, she hoped with all her heart that it was Zaandr on Pog's back.

Pog leapt from the window, but just as he did, the building behind him gave a groaning shudder. The walls cracked and came apart, lingering in the air for a fraction of a heartbeat before collapsing with a roar as if they were alive and being torn apart. Smoke and dust rushed up in a billowing cloud, as Tegan was pierced through with blinding pain that wrenched a tortured scream from her lips.

NINETEEN

Tegan sank to her knees as the building collapsed into a pile of smoking rubble. A sob escaped her lips as she fought not to let despair consume her, but she couldn't sense Zaandr anymore. She'd never been able to read him like he could her, but she'd enjoyed the faint hum of his emotions mingling with hers. Now, she couldn't feel anything.

"Vrax!" Tori called after the Dothvek as he ran toward the remains of the building, but he didn't slow. She growled, scowling at her mate's back. "Stubborn Dothvek." Then she raced in after him, her wild curls flying behind her like a mane.

"This is my fault," Tegan said, as Rose crouched with her on the ground. "I cursed him."

"Are you a witch?" Rose asked.

Tegan shook her head. "He was fine before he met me. I was fine before I met him. But this is what happens when you care too much." She waved a hand at the smoldering rubble. "If you care about someone too much, they leave. They run away, or they die, but it never ends up well. It's a curse."

Rose gave a sad shake of her head. "Loving someone isn't a curse, and none of this is your fault."

Tegan's scratchy throat constricted. "I didn't even tell him...before I left him in that burning house. I couldn't tell him."

Rose put an arm around her shoulders. "I don't think you needed to. Anyone with eyes could see how crazy you were for him."

Rose's words didn't make Tegan didn't feel any better. She should have told Zaandr, but she'd been scared of exactly what had happened. It had been too fast and too real, and it had petrified her.

No matter how hard Tegan had tried to shield herself, she had still been left broken hearted. She had still lost him. She had still been left alone.

More Dothveks appeared, running toward the smoking remains of the building, along with residents of Kurril, who appeared with buckets of water to douse the flames still burning. Even the wounded resistance fighter was pawing through the rubble with her one uninjured arm.

Tegan pushed herself to her feet. She couldn't fall apart. Not when Zaandr and Rixx were in there somewhere. She gave Rose a hug and thanked her as Cat rushed up to her, and her two Dothvek mates kept running toward the wreckage.

"We heard," she said, as she caught her breath, motioning to her head. "Well, the Dothveks heard like they do."

"They felt us all the way from the ship?"

Cat shook her head. "Not felt. They got a call for help—from Zaandr."

Tegan's heart stuttered in her chest. Zaandr had sent a mental message to his Dothvek brothers for help? "When?"

"I don't know. As long ago as it takes to run full-out from the shipyard. All the guys got it and took off."

Tegan hadn't sensed any call for help, but she wasn't Dothvek. Plus, she'd been in a state of panic and distress. She didn't know how Dothvek mind reading worked, but she was sure her near hysteria didn't make it easier.

Then she spotted a flash of green. She waved her hands in front of her to dissipate the smoke as she walked toward the green, expecting to see a bird with lots of feathers. Instead, there was a green creature with a long trunk spurting water at the fire.

"Pog!" She rushed to him, her gaze scouring the area surrounding him. "Where's Zaandr and Rixx? Where's the Dothvek who was on your back?"

"That's Pog?" Cat asked, blinking rapidly, as she pushed her curly hair from her face. "Are you sure?"

Pog swung his trunk and blasted water onto a limp, gold-skinned body a few steps away.

Tegan shrieked as the figure jerked up and coughed. She ran to Zaandr and threw her arms around him. "You're alive!"

"And wet." Zaandr spit out a mouthful of water as he pushed himself up to sitting "Why am I wet?"

Tegan laughed. "Pog transformed into some kind of creature with a trunk, and he's dousing the fire with water."

"We really should get a few more Pogs."

"I thought you were still inside the building." Tegan's voice broke as she ran her hands over his damp skin, as if to make sure he was real. "We didn't see if Pog made it out, or who was on his back."

"I was on his back." Zaandr's eyes closed for a beat. "Rixx insisted I go first. He said you had something you needed to tell me when I got down."

Tegan's vision blurred. "He was right. I should have told you before I left with Pog, but I was scared and stupid."

He brushed a strand of hair from her forehead. "You are far from stupid, but I understand why you were scared."

She pressed a hand to his chest. "I'm not scared anymore. I know you'd never willingly leave me. I don't want to lose you because I'm afraid. I can't lose you."

He pinned her with an intense gaze. "Then don't."

She exhaled a shaky breath. "I won't.

"You're right that I would never leave you." He put his hand on top of hers and squeezed. "I promise."

Tegan nodded, a tear snaking down one cheek. "I believe you." She put a hand to his cheek, almost unable to believe the strength of her emotions. It should be impossible to fall for someone so quickly, but her feelings for him were real and powerful. She'd never felt as sure about anything in her life as she did about him, and she'd spent most of her life being sure that she would never love anyone. She had never been so glad to be so wrong as she was in that moment. "I love you."

I know. He captured her mouth in a soft kiss that deepened as he tangled a hand in her hair.

When he pulled back, she smiled. "I have to confess something."

Zaandr cocked his head to one side.

She flicked her gaze to the Lycithian shape-shifter who was putting out the smoldering fire. "I also love Pog."

The Dothvek gave her a crooked grin. "Don't we all?"

CHAPTER
TWENTY

Once Tegan was convinced he was okay and had left him to talk to Rose, Zaandr made his way to where Vrax was searching the smoldering rubble. Pog's dousing of the flames with water had extinguished the fire, but it had left everything waterlogged. Part of the back walls stood, creating a blackened shell, and the roof had partially caved in, but still hung over part of the debris.

Vrax nudged a charred body with one foot. "This looks like a Zevrian."

Zaandr bent over and eyed the body, recognizing the clothing and leather armor that one of the aliens had worn. He grunted. "I think I killed him."

His stomach twisted as he looked at the burned corpse. Was Rixx's scorched body under the rubble? He couldn't sense him, but that could mean that he was unconscious. Zaandr refused to believe that his best friend was dead until they found evidence, and so far, there was none.

"He might have escaped." Zaandr spotted the twin warriors digging in the wreckage along with K'alvek, and he sensed their frustration along with the bits of hope they clung to like rafts on a turbulent sea.

Vrax nodded absently. "Why can't we feel him?"

Zaandr frowned. He had no answer for that. He should be able to sense his friend. Of all the Dothveks, he'd always been most tightly bonded to Rixx. If he couldn't sense his emotions or thoughts, that meant he was unconscious. He gulped. Or dead.

He shook his head, refusing to believe it. Rixx was a survivor.

Vrax cut a glance to him. "You going to tell me the whole story, and how all this happened?"

Zaandr considered everything that had taken place in the pleasure house run by the underground resistance, his mind revisiting his night with Tegan.

Vrax head up his hands. "Never mind. Even though we're related, there are some things I don't need to know."

Zaandr appreciated that his kinsman didn't insist on a full explanation, although he knew all the Dothveks had picked up on his sudden connection to Tegan. Since they'd all taken mates who weren't from their home world, they understood better than most what it was like to fall under the spell of humans—or in Vrax's case, a Zevrian.

"I owe you and Tegan an apology." Vrax sighed deeply. "And most of all, Rixx. The only reason any of this happened was because the Zevrians were still bitter over how things ended when Tori and I were on Kurril. It didn't occur to me that enough of them would have remained here, or that they'd take Rixx thinking he was me."

Zaandr patted the Dothvek's shoulder. "The only ones who deserve blame for this are the Zevrians."

Vrax's guilt and regret pulsed off him in waves. "I should

have been the one taken and the one..." His voice trailed off as he surveyed the rubble.

"He is not dead," Zaandr said with more force than he felt.

He couldn't bear to think that his friend had sacrificed himself so that Zaandr could survive and be with Tegan. When they'd been standing together in the window and acrid smoke had been making it hard to speak, Rixx had refused to go first, even though he was the one who'd been held captive and was injured. His friend had given Zaandr a hard, fast hug and told him that he needed to go first.

"You have someone waiting for you, Zaandr, and unless I've lost my touch at reading females, she has something she wants to tell you." When Zaandr had hesitated, his friend had given him a shove. "If you don't get on the back of this green chicken, I'm going to push you out the window myself."

Zaandr's throat had been tight as he'd gotten on Pog's back, and the goodbye between them had felt more final than he had wanted it to feel.

But Rixx had slapped Pog on the rump and forced himself to smile through the coughing. *I'm right behind you, brother.*

Then Pog had leapt into the air, unfurled his wings, and the building had emitted a deafening roar behind them moments before it collapsed.

"It is not your fault either." Vrax's voice snapped him back to the present, and Zaandr realized that the Dothvek had been sensing his thoughts.

"He should be here. We came here to rescue *him*."

A sense of dread washed over him, and Vrax's face contorted as he obviously felt the same thing. They both looked over to where the twin Dothveks Dev and Trek were standing over something, their expressions somber. Zaandr stopped breathing as grief sunk its sharp talons into his heart.

Rixx.

TWENTY-ONE

T egan looked up when Zaandr entered their quarters.
"Any luck?"

Since returning to the ship, she and the Dothvek
had made their bonding public, and had been given a large
room to share. She'd thought it would be strange to suddenly
share quarters with a guy—and one so large—but they'd
adjusted to living together without much fuss. Of course,
Zaandr had spent almost every waking moment searching for
his friend.

The Dothvek shook his head, kicked off his boots, and
flopped onto their bed. "We pawed through every bit of the
rubble, and I'm not convinced any of the bodies are Rixx. No
matter what the others think."

She stood from the desk where she'd been making notes
about the various pregnant females on board and updating her
estimates on their due dates. "And you still can't sense him?"

Zaandr scowled and didn't answer.

"There are lots of reasons you might not be picking up on
his thoughts," Tegan said, even though she didn't fully believe

what she was saying. "The Den of Thieves isn't exactly quiet. Between the crowds and the criminals, the emotions must be a mess to sort through."

"They are," Zaandr admitted, "but I should have picked up something by now."

Tegan sat next to him on the edge of the bed and rested a hand on his leg. "You and the others have done everything possible to find him."

Zaandr scraped a hand through his long hair. "It's like he vanished into thin air."

From what Tegan had heard, if there was any place you could disappear without a trace, it was Kurril, although usually those who disappeared were trying not to be found. Rixx had no reason to hide from his fellow Dothveks.

She believed Zaandr when he said that the bodies they'd found weren't his friend, even though some had been burned so badly it was impossible to discern any features. If he believed Rixx was alive, then so did she. Still, she knew his faith in finding his friend was flagging.

"But you'll keep looking, right?"

A low sound rumbled from Zaandr's throat. "We can't. K'alvek heard the guards at the shipyard gate say that a Zevrian fleet is approaching. If they're looking for the ones who are responsible for the death of their people, we can't be anywhere near here when they arrive."

As if on cue, the ship's engines rumbled to life.

"I have some good news," Tegan said, changing the subject without much grace and hoping to distract Zaandr.

He cocked an eyebrow at her.

"You know when you said we needed more Pogs?" She scooped up Pog from where the Lycithian pet had been sleeping on the bed. "Your wish is about to come true. Pog is pregnant!"

Zaandr stared at her. "Pog is a he."

She shook her head. "That's what I thought, but Bexli told me that Lycithian glurkins are actually neither male nor female, and they reproduce asexually. The other day I felt some lumps in Pog's belly and did a sonogram. Our little shape-shifting friend is expecting three babies."

"So he is a they?" Zaandr slid his gaze to the creature, who was purring in Tegan's arms. "Three babies? I hope they aren't going to be staying here." Then he grinned. "Does Tori know?"

It was common knowledge that the Zevrian made a big show about being annoyed by Pog.

Tegan grinned. "She only pretends not to like Pog. Maybe we can convince her to adopt one of the poglings."

Zaandr grinned and ruffled Pog's fur. "After how he, I mean they, saved us, I can't say I'm sorry that we'll have more." He looped an arm around Tegan. "It isn't as exciting as expecting a baby of our own, but I'll take any good news."

Tegan's stomach fluttered. "I don't mind the idea of being a mother myself anymore, but I'm guessing it will be a while until we have a baby."

Zaandr pulled her onto his lap so that she was straddling him. "I would say that's too bad, but this just gives us an excuse to keep trying."

She laughed and swatted at him, another flutter dancing in her stomach. "What did I tell you about needing to be able to walk?"

He pulled her down so he could nuzzle her neck. "And what did I say about being willing to carry you everywhere?"

Before she could tell him that he was being ridiculous, she sensed something that made her breath hitch in her throat. "What was that?"

"Hmmm?" Zaandr murmured into her throat.

"I felt something." Tegan's heart raced. "A pulse of emotion that wasn't yours."

Zaandr pulled back and frowned. "Another Dothvek?"

She shook her head, suddenly knowing without a doubt what she'd felt. "No. It's coming from...inside me."

Zaandr glanced down at her belly, his jaw dropping. "I thought you said..."

"I guess I was wrong." Tears choked Tegan's voice as the certainty sunk in. She was carrying Zaandr's baby. "I hope you're ready to be a dad."

"More ready than you can imagine," he husked, before capturing her mouth in a kiss that made her stomach do another happy flip.

EPILOGUE

Rixx groaned as he woke. His head throbbed, and his side twinged as he attempted to raise a hand to his temple. Breathing in, he was startled not to be inhaling bitter smoke. His last memory had been of breathing in acrid air that seared his lungs as he stood on the windowsill. Zaandr had left on Pog's back. He'd felt the building rumble beneath his feet. He'd made the split-second decision to leap from the window. Then everything behind him had exploded, and his world had gone black.

He gingerly opened his eyes, expecting to see blackened rubble overhead. Instead, there were the pristine, wooden beams of a low ceiling. Not burned and not collapsed. There was no hint of a fire, and the only aroma was that of something savory. His stomach rumbled in response.

Had he imagined the fire, and Zaandr rescuing him with Tegan and a very different looking Pog? Had that been some sort of fever dream? Was he still being held by the Zevrians who enjoyed coming in every so often and beating him? Had he passed out from the pain? Was he dreaming this?

If so, he much preferred this dream to the one in which he feared the heat of the nearing flames. In this dream, there was a soft voice humming and a warm blanket covering him. Rixx sighed deeply, sinking further into the dream, and hoping it would never end.

"You shouldn't move too much. We don't want your wounds to tear again."

His eyes opened as the face of a female came into view. A human female with dark hair braided and wrapped in a bun on top of her head. He didn't recognize her or understand why he would insert a mystery human in his imaginings. Then he attempted to sit up and pain shot through him. He collapsed back onto the bed with a gasp. This was no dream.

"You aren't a very good listener, are you?" The woman made clucking sounds of disapproval as she touched her hands gently to his side. "If you try to move too much, you'll open your wound, and you've already lost too much blood."

His head swam as the pain faded. "Who are you?"

The woman smiled at him. "My name is Myrria." Then she tilted her head. "I could ask you the same thing, since I found you slumped in my doorway and covered in soot."

He frowned as he tried to remember this. He had no memory of anything beyond leaping from the building in which he'd been held captive. "You live in the Den of Thieves?"

She nodded, her expression darkening for a beat. "My husband brought us here. He said it was a place for people who were blessed with luck."

Rixx scanned the small room and peered through the open archway into a larger, common room. He saw no one else.

As if sensing his confusion, the woman pursed her lips. "I was not blessed by luck. My husband joined the crew of a ship, and he never returned."

"He left you alone?" This was unthinkable to him. Why

would a male leave his mate and take a dangerous voyage on a spaceship?

"Not all alone. I have a daughter." She flicked her gaze to a small head peeking around the corner of the archway.

Rixx met her gaze. "And you took me in? A single woman and her child?"

Myrria lifted her chin. "If you're asking if I was afraid of you, no. You were so wounded when I found you, my daughter could have fought you and won."

Rixx laughed, but the pain in his side stopped him. "Then I owe you a debt of gratitude."

"Kurril is not a kind place to strangers or the weak and injured." She shook her head. "I know that too well. If I hadn't brought you in, they would have stripped your body for organs or thrown you into the fighting pits as bait. Someone was kind to me here once. I am paying that kindness forward."

"You will be well rewarded when I am returned to my ship." Rixx's head was clearing now. "I came here with a crew of Dothveks and bounty hunters."

A glimmer of recognition sparkled in her eyes. "I don't venture out much, but I did hear of some gold-skinned aliens who arrived on the planet." Then her face fell. "But their ship departed."

"Departed? They left?" He reached out his mind and found no trace of Dothvek thought.

She nodded. "Many days ago."

"Days?" His voice cracked. How long had he been unconscious? "I have to get word to them that I'm alive."

"Not if you want to remain alive." She dropped her voice and glanced at the shuttered window, as if someone was listening in to their conversation. "As soon as the bounty hunter ship left, a fleet of Zevrians arrived, and they've been searching the city for any clues as to where it went or the aliens who crew it. They are hunting for Dothveks." She shivered. "They are hunting for you."

Rixx closed his eyes. He was stranded on Kurril with a fleet of Zevrians hunting him and no way to escape. When he'd left his home world looking for adventure, this had *not* been what he'd had in mind.

Thank you for reading RESCUE! If you'd like to read a bonus scene with Tegan and Zaandr (and meet the new poglings), click below to join my VIP Reader group and get the bonus scene!

https://BookHip.com/PNWKCVL

Also by Tana Stone

The Barbarians of the Sand Planet Series:

BOUNTY (also available in AUDIO)

CAPTIVE (also available in AUDIO)

TORMENT (also available on AUDIO)

TRIBUTE (also available as AUDIO)

SAVAGE (also available in AUDIO)

CLAIM (also available on AUDIO)

CHERISH: A Holiday Baby Short (also available on AUDIO)

PRIZE (also available on AUDIO)

SECRET

RESCUE

GUARD

Warriors of the Drexian Academy:

LEGACY

LOYALTY

OBSESSION

LEGEND

SECRECY

REVENGE

Inferno Force of the Drexian Warriors:

IGNITE (also available on AUDIO)

SCORCH (also available on AUDIO)

BURN (also available on AUDIO)

BLAZE (also available on AUDIO)

FLAME (also available on AUDIO)

COMBUST (also available on AUDIO)

The Tribute Brides of the Drexian Warriors Series:

TAMED (also available in AUDIO)

SEIZED (also available in AUDIO)

EXPOSED (also available in AUDIO)

RANSOMED (also available in AUDIO)

FORBIDDEN (also available in AUDIO)

BOUND (also available in AUDIO)

JINGLED (A Holiday Novella) (also in AUDIO)

CRAVED (also available in AUDIO)

STOLEN (also available in AUDIO)

SCARRED (also available in AUDIO)

ALIEN & MONSTER ONE-SHOTS:

ROGUE (also available in AUDIO)

VIXIN: STRANDED WITH AN ALIEN

SLIPPERY WHEN YETI

CHRISTMAS WITH AN ALIEN

YOOL

DAD BOD ORC

Raider Warlords of the Vandar Series:

POSSESSED (also available in AUDIO)

PLUNDERED (also available in AUDIO)

PILLAGED (also available in AUDIO)

PURSUED (also available in AUDIO)

PUNISHED (also available on AUDIO)

PROVOKED (also available in AUDIO)

PRODIGAL (also available in AUDIO)

PRISONER

PROTECTOR

PRINCE

THE SKY CLAN OF THE TAORI:

SUBMIT (also available in AUDIO)

STALK (also available on AUDIO)

SEDUCE (also available on AUDIO)

SUBDUE

STORM

All the TANA STONE books available as audiobooks!

INFERNO FORCE OF THE DREXIAN WARRIORS:

IGNITE on AUDIBLE

SCORCH on AUDIBLE

BURN on AUDIBLE

BLAZE on AUDIBLE

FLAME on AUDIBLE

RAIDER WARLORDS OF THE VANDAR:

POSSESSED on AUDIBLE

PLUNDERED on AUDIBLE

PILLAGED on AUDIBLE

PURSUED on AUDIBLE

PUNISHED on AUDIBLE

PROVOKED on AUDIBLE

BARBARIANS OF THE SAND PLANET

BOUNTY on AUDIBLE

CAPTIVE on AUDIBLE

TORMENT on AUDIBLE

TRIBUTE on AUDIBLE

SAVAGE on AUDIBLE

CLAIM on AUDIBLE

CHERISH on AUDIBLE

TRIBUTE BRIDES OF THE DREXIAN WARRIORS

TAMED on AUDIBLE

SEIZED on AUDIBLE

EXPOSED on AUDIBLE

RANSOMED on AUDIBLE

FORBIDDEN on AUDIBLE

BOUND on AUDIBLE

JINGLED on AUDIBLE

CRAVED on AUDIBLE

STOLEN on AUDIBLE

SCARRED on AUDIBLE

SKY CLAN OF THE TAORI

SUBMIT on AUDIBLE

STALK on AUDIBLE

SEDUCE on AUDIBLE

About the Author

Tana Stone is a bestselling sci-fi romance author who loves sexy aliens and independent heroines. Her favorite superhero is Thor (with Aquaman a close second because, well, Jason Momoa), her favorite dessert is key lime pie (okay, fine, *all* pie), and she loves Star Wars and Star Trek equally. She still laments the loss of *Firefly*.

She has one husband, two teenagers, and two neurotic cats. She sometimes wishes she could teleport to a holographic space station like the one in her tribute brides series (or maybe vacation at the oasis with the sand planet barbarians). :-)

She loves hearing from readers! Email her any questions or comments at tana@tanastone.com.

Want to hang out with Tana in her private Facebook group? Join on all the fun at: https://www.facebook.com/groups/tanastonestributes/

Made in the USA
Columbia, SC
27 July 2024